Alive,
I Cried
Fiercely

Alive, I Cried Fiercely

A Jonah Experience...
An Amazing Adventure Inside That Monstrous Beast

TOMMY R. BANKS, SR

Copyright © Tommy R. Banks, Sr.

All rights reserved. No part of this book may be reproduced in any form or by any electronic or mechanical means, including information storage and retrieval systems, without permission in writing from the publisher, except by reviewers, who may quote brief passages in a review.

ISBN: 978-1-63649-971-0 (Paperback Edition)
ISBN: 978-1-63649-972-7 (Hardcover Edition)
ISBN: 978-1-63649-970-3 (E-book Edition)

Some characters and events in this book are fictitious. Any similarity to real persons, living or dead, is coincidental and not intended by the author.

The author guarantees all contents are original and do not infringe upon the legal rights of any other person or work. No portion of this book may be reproduced, stored in a retrieval system, or transmitted in any form or by any means—electronic, mechanical, photocopy, recording, scanning, or other—except for brief quotations in critical reviews or articles, without the prior written permission of the author. The author assumes full responsibility for the accuracy of all facts and quotations as cited in this book. The views expressed in this book are not necessarily those of the publisher.

Notes and quotations credited to my spiritual inheritance from the divine Holy Spirit of God; and from both of my books:

Youthology, Copyright © 2010 by Tommy R. Banks, Sr., ISBN 9781615798803.

Dangerous Crossing- Look, Listen, and Live, copyright © 2013 by Tommy R. Banks, Sr., Registration Number TX 7-911-343 May 14, 2014, ISBN 9781449793890.

Unless otherwise indicated, Bible Texts credited to KJV are from the well-worn Holy Bible, King James Version, copyright © 1975 by Thomas Nelson Inc., Publishers Nashville, Tennessee.

Book Ordering Information

Phone Number: 315 288-7939 ext. 1000 or 347-901-4920
Email: info@globalsummithouse.com
Global Summit House
www.globalsummithouse.com

Printed in the United States of America

To my dear wife and much-loved son,
whom I sincerely love and who faithfully serve our
only Lord and Savior, Jesus Christ, our precious family,
and the faithful church of our God together.
Wanda, as Lady B
Tommy, as PK

CONTENTS

Introduction xi

Chapter 1: Disobedience: "The Young Fugitive" 1
Chapter 2: A Decade Of Sin 13
Chapter 3: The Great Storm 37
Chapter 4: The Pursuit Of Joy 50
Chapter 5: Obedience: "When The Lord Commands,
    Do It With Impunity" 57

Biography 77
Jonah: God's (Selfish) Prophet 79
Annotations 81
Author's Prayer: (From My Heart Dedicated to Yours,
    In Jesus' Name) 83
Author's Poem: (In the Big—Bulky Whale Alive, I Cried) 85
Self-Love and Practical Self-Responsibility 87
Preface 89
Dedication 91
Acknowledgments: (Thanks To) 93
About The Author 95
About the Book 97
Look for these Other Books By Tommy R. Banks, Sr. 99

INTRODUCTION

(For it is in New Castle Town that our scene lies)

Narrator Talks (Via the Leading Protagonist Thomas Blueberry, a. k. a. Mister Big Tom):

The Lifetime Memories of a Paranormal Experience:

(I was thirty-seven.) It was an unbearably sultry summer bloom. And no other day was like that terrible time. Now the dear Lord had prepared an enormous beast to swallow up a jolly, long-married man who chose a selfish path. And for the past three miserable days and three sleepless nights, which he lay in agony in the high-flying belly of the mighty monster. And now he must suffer and sincerely mourn while on the undefeated run from God.

Temporarily, they have eagerly snatched this rebellious family man away into the incredible depths of the dark deep-sea. And it gently washed his pleasant memory out by overflowing water and deepening gloom that crumbled over him. So even though it precious was a pleasant half-hour before local noon, he floats aimlessly about the watery doom of New Castle Town. In the visible vein of a tropical summer day in late June, along with the fiery sun glaring down upon him from above.

And yet, Mister Big Tom has instantly remembered with personal regret. For the first meaningful time since that blistering day, he was balky: full of a compelling argument. As he steadfastly refused to obey God's direct command to go out on the dirty streets of New Castle Town. And preach the good news of the Kingdom of God to all the precious people of that leading city, for they remain the wicked enemies of God.

The dear people lived in the unholy city (noted for its large magnificent buildings, with tall solid walls) and were happy to stay there. Just as long as they can do whatever they want. And there will not be any consequences for their willful disobedience of that which God's word declares as foolishness.

The Time after Midnight:

One day in the morning of noon during the supernatural encounter with God (The first time God spoke to him in a personal way.) And he was walking through the narrow footpath beside the Old Little Rock Road. While gently lowering his shapely head and reminiscing kindly a personal bit about the authoritative voice, he had undoubtedly heard; and so, after a few breathless seconds of more gloomy thoughts and more of his rebellious ways.

Then, all at once, the defiant and uncooperative isolated gent looking up (toward the pearly sky) at the Son of God for direct answers to his dear life. And then, suddenly, his naughty thoughts carry him down to and through those big blue waves in the mighty ocean of his dearly loved soul; like the runaway energy, that floats now and on into eternity; and then, all of a sudden, his invisible spirit leaps to a shiny light. And then, he suddenly woke up (His memories back!) He then begins to relive his life with intact memories of his previous living; until, despite his best efforts at intentionally disregarding God's divine command, in which he immediately rejected.

I Don't Want To Be A Prophet:

"The idea of fortunetelling scares me."
"Maybe I'm not good enough."
"They won't listen to me."
"I'm going to sound stupid," said thoughtfully him.

Mister Big Tom makes known that the only thing he knew about prophets, was what he had heard in Sunday-school and Bible-study: prophets were weird, dressed in animal skins and always shouting about the coming destruction. It is undoubtedly just his moral imagination, that ability to honestly think of being true to God that needs to be activated.

I mean morally (after all), he could have refused to face the facts about himself as many of us do today. When a hasty glance at our own lives. It credibly threatens to make us uncomfortable, and we often look at ourselves for some moral good deed to put our conscious mind at ease. But the most leading character, Thomas Blueberry politely tells us that of which he could never think without a quicker beating of the dear heart. He immediately thought, and through his stunning disquietedness passed out of a beautiful summer day, into a dark and dreadful sleepless night.

The Next Day He's A Grumpy Renegade:

On the following morning, it's a gloomy and unpleasant day. And Mister Big Tom faithfully represents a moody, cantankerous unmarried man with a small and somewhat ridiculous beard. He's running merrily from his spiritual preaching journey. And everything instantly started desperately happening in his modern life.

It begins fiercely with a life-death situation, involving a mighty, sightless beast with an oversized monster's flowing tail; which proves both wise and gentle. And a miserable thief, "whose name is Tuff," whispered gently the humble narrator, a terrible miscreant. When at first, he intentionally tries to rob the main character at gunpoint but ends up being the vulnerable victim.

Tuff is very much shocked by the illuminating power of what he indeed heard from the leading character. And positively agree to the eternal truth of the glorious gospel as it's just been preached.

Meanwhile, Thomas Blueberry stood with his grateful hands hoisted in the sultry air. Finally, after a long and uncomfortable silence, he said thoughtfully with quiet intensity, making eye contact, and his excellent choice of sacred words came as a divine revelation from his recent past and his distant future. His mild voice hardened as he spoke more rapidly using a simple mantra:

> *"Tuff, come now, don't waste any more time! Stop here and don't be a thief that winds up in Hell! You must follow Yahweh and do whatever He tells you!!"*

Unsurprisingly, the leading character uttered to the so-called robber armed with a small loaded handgun. Aiming merely to kill instantly (Mister Big Tom's divine message was clear as a cold slap in Tuff's passionless face).

Wow, The Odds Shift Radically:

But when successful conversion naturally comes to Tuff, the tables turn dramatically in his strong-arm robbery attempt. As he shrugged his shoulders and willingly surrendered his loaded Judas gun (.38 Special). Just before taking off and landing in the cobblestone streets of New Castle Town. And now, he's by faithful heart a whole new person, a jolly man blessed by God's eternal truth.

Amazingly, Tuff more thoroughly believes Jesus remains undoubtedly his faithful Lord. As he sufficiently learns to properly recognize God and works towards to live peacefully with Him.

It is in fact, quite the exact opposite of what Tuff at likely first believed. In the middle of his wicked life; for a rare instance, Tuff naturally thought his destructive behavior was truly a divine blessing of God, but now he sincerely believes this is not really a spiritual gift. Instead, it's more of a terrible curse than a mighty miracle, because he had sinned significantly and fell short of the dear Lord's everlasting glory.

Since then, Tuff has willingly accepted God's divine gift of eternal salvation through Mister Big Tom's actions, thoughts, and dialogue. The inspired word transformed in Tuff's moved heart, that thief turned from evil to good, or at least into a more Christ-like character. He relies on that word of prophecy for support when he tries convincing the main character into answering his divine calling:

popularly known as the Great Commission because it is a command to share the grace of Christ with the entire world.

But while Mister Big Tom is steadfastly refusing to acknowledge God's supreme authority to serve as a holy man. And speak to all the precious people of New Castle Town, for they continue being the unrighteous enemies of God. And now, he's intentionally missing and in fearful danger.

In The Meantime:

Narrator Talks Continue (Via the Leading Character):

However, Mister Big Tom is mysteriously abducted temporarily into a deep ocean of overflowing water, but not to be killed by drowning.

As a viable substitute, he wakes up traumatized inside the prominent belly of a mighty, sightless beast with deepening dreadful gloom and visible smoke that crumbled over him. And with hideous noises that sound like someone crying horribly.

He is also unmarried and living with personal regret outside the noble city in an uncomfortably narrow and muddy-looking (upper-story) Castle house; accessible by the incredibly dry, sultry desert air, with a deteriorating staircase; featured cedar-wood construction and a bluish-white metal roof, with its blank walls ivy-sand (upon which was very bare); and was merely furnished with an old beat-up pale-brown Naugahyde wood sofa.

"I'm afraid," I said timidly.

"I'm really, really hot in this shotgun house; filled with creepy, slimy substance that shrunk (like squishy walls sagging) from my lively touch."

"I'm falling apart."

"I'm barely breathing,"

Although I am all along with my big and bulky Bible: a thick, quarto-sized stacked book with a black back and a leather cover. Its well-worn pages were rough and craggy. And I don't know what to do in ninety-five soundless feet of murky water. While being separated from the forgotten rest of the dear world as continuous daylight shattered away.

Feeling genuinely shocked and terribly confused, I rushed back to work in New Castle Town, but no one supposedly knows me; not even my closest friends gratefully recognize me.

The Good-Hearted Bad Man:

Confused, I run desperately to the cobbled street and encounter the affirmed gunman, Tuff. Who is now a born-again Christian with a dark, baleful past: Tuff is indeed a former hired gun, the most lethal Southerner assassin ever created. After decades of violent work, the dear Lord, Tuff says graciously with his eager hands in the sultry air like a Pentecostal praising God; who had blessed him with spiritual joy and lasting peace; who has miraculously delivered him from indescribably evil, especially when He faithfully redeemed Tuff from mortal sin and all terrible kinds of portentous crimes?

Meantime, Tuff faithfully continues relating the inspirational story of God's divine grace and his salvation to Mister Big Tom. In an unbelievable episode; Tuff talks about a remarkable account of divine miracles, miraculous healings, and life inside the private world of New Castle Town.

Upon which he gently said: God, the Savior, has been good to me; but most of all when he faithfully delivered me from my terrible misfortunes. Therefore, you willingly see, when God politely tells you to go carefully in a certain direction; don't turn back. God's unmistakable way is always best. If you fully obey God and carefully follow all his lovely commands, he will heartily rejoice in willingly doing you good. "And (incidentally) God will bless you at all precious times. In everything you undoubtedly do," said thoughtfully Tuff, and he believed it; and that belief set his heart palpitating.

"Unsurprisingly, the Lord God will bless you just as He willingly promised you."

After that, Tuff, politely, tells Mister Big Tom about how he suffered tremendously the horrific atrocity knowingly committed by arrested Thursday's local killer. Ironically, known as Old Blue, Tuff's former cellmate (He was naturally born in Big Foot, Arkansas, but moved to New Castle Town; where they grew up in foster homes.) They voluntarily attended West Castle High School here in New

Castle Town. Shortly before the promising start of his recent faith life, Old Blue was in question for knowingly killing a young boy named Jack Reston ("He was the most sensible, quiet, clever young boy you would ever want to meet," Tuff told Mister Big Tom.)

Murder by Mistake:

("I Didn't Mean To Do It")

So finally when he got to the mall, Old Blue took his gun inside the New Castle Town's Greenway Plaza, telling police it accidentally fired.

"Oh, I accidentally shot Jack in the chest."

"Why in God's name you do that??" the chief officer said.

"Well, I didn't mean to do it. It was an accident!"

"Tuff said Old Blue was going to get in a fight with four bad guys. And his gun accidentally discharged, shooting Jack through the chest so that he afterward died."

Tuff also said he remember a young Jack Reston who didn't have many friends. Since his death, many junior boys have claimed that they have been Jack's friends. "I know for a fact that wasn't true," Tuff said.

Therefore, Tuff wraps up his rambling conversations with Mister Big Tom by telling him that Old Blue has a heavy dose of guilt to burden him. And while he regrets everything that happened; he wishes he can carefully undo his wrongs. I spoke with him sometimes, and he really feels disappointed.

Finally, Mister Big Tom spoke. His voice crackled (like a whip, full of heat and command), "But do you remember our conversation on that one dreadful day about late afternoon, some seventy-two hours ago?" Mister Big Tom asked, looking at Tuff suspiciously.

"Yes, very well," Tuff said gratefully. You were right, God does love me."

On top of that, God naturally wants us to have eternal joy and to become more like him. "All the same, Mister Big Tom, sincerely thank you for willingly sharing the Good News (i.e. the Gospel, nearly too precious good to be true news) of Jesus Christ with me.

For instantly reminding me and gently encouraging my dear heart, over and over again. That it's all about the unconditional love of God, which is precisely in Jesus Christ our dear Lord."

"My fulfilled prophecy was so, so, so, so right on! Sincerely thank you, thank you, and thank you."

Narrator Talks (Via the Gunman Tuff):

In the meantime, Tuff carefully explains that Mister Big Tom is typically undergoing a traumatic experience, cloistered inside the prominent belly of a large whale. He is constantly tormented in divine order to learn a lesson that is personal to Mister Big Tom's spiritual life.

As a direct result, Tuff earnestly advises Mister Big Tom to take the time to discover whatever it is that he dearly needs to naturally learn.

Narrator Talks Continue:

After a great deal of reasoning; and now, Thomas Blueberry instantly realizes he's single and living with personal regret the lively life that he definitely does not want to live.

As a possible substitute, he is precisely a poor and destitute pawnshop salesman, who suffers greatly at the present time; only if he had not refused to willingly follow the dear Lord.

But nevertheless, he undoubtedly enjoys an exceptional family life (Which in fact, he misses very, very much!) Where he is an industrial executive of the NCT Industrial Direction, Incorporation; authorized retailer of industrial products including tools, hardware, fittings, valves, and materials. Thomas Blueberry's chosen profession has been faithfully related to active management and industrial relations. His peaceful job from the very beginning has been carefully helping dispirited people find themselves through positive thinking.

Though he has never acknowledged openly the divine call of God's Spirit, he has been influenced by the well-worn Holy Bible, God's Words and Scriptures. Which were available in English translation, especially those of the original Hebrews language like the Books of the Old and New Testament?

All the same, he's been wonderfully married for almost ten successful years this July. With one amazing kid and his dear wife, lovely Mrs. Liaduia, a fifth-grade school teacher (at New Castle Town Elementary, who specializes in modern mathematics).

Narrator Talks (Via Mr. Big Tom's Wife, Mrs. Liaduia)**:**

He Loves Me, He Loves Me Not:

For the past three radiant days and three sultry nights, I was living harmoniously a consistent cycle of arguing persuasively and crying, instantly putting myself into dangerous situations and feeling alone and confused. Every successful attempt that I naturally made to carefully help my dear husband seemed to fail spectacularly.

"Oh, well, I hope his life gets better and less cantankerous."

"He certainly must either find gentle grace or be forced to it," said wistfully dear Mrs. Liaduia at completed last; indeed, he must.

"Therefore, trust and obey Him, my dear love as your God and your Lord and Savior; pray if you can, we too are praying for you."

The Main Character Talks:

Soon after that, my young son, Little Tom instantly realizes my divine secret, naturally thinks I am a removable alien but a friendly one. And voluntarily decide to help me in miraculously surviving my former life.

But as a terrible replacement, I am a lonely, pawnshop salesman. I am undoubtedly having a real hard time dealing harshly with my alternative life (Instantly lost in a dark and deep sea of untold miseries that made me feel like I might drown in despair.) Therefore, it is difficult and unpleasant for me to deal in my past experience at the New Castle Town. And with all of whom I was personally well acquainted to.

TOMMY R. BANKS, SR.

Things Fall Apart:

("New Castle Town Ten Years Earlier")

In the present climate, ten years up to now, I naturally suffer an incredible lack of emotional empathy but am pummeled by my active imagination. I am twenty-seven years old. I struggle hard to fit into the leading role of a faithful, unmarried, reasonable man. I am mindless, cares little about anyone except me, and making bad many serious goofs like flirting with lots of party girls; going out with friends and dear co-workers, day by day and night by night; hitting the bars and restaurants, night and day, no time for work, no time to pray; drinking like fish (As a negative result of which, I stumbled awkwardly in place, hollering catchwords which only my dear friends instantly understood; laughing uproariously) most of my own accord. And we danced like sparkling stars (Everybody's dancing in a joyous ring around the radiant sun. So hey Mr. Deejay let the music play.) We're gonna cheerfully dance, boogie, till the morning light. "And we're gonna party like its nineteen ninety-nine, but only it's not," cried Mister Big Tom joyously.

"We're going to merrily dance, dance, and dance this life away!"

I joyfully celebrate in the most fearful time of my glorious years. Though I had heartily despised the gentle voice of the Lord, I am confident that God will not despise me.

Under those circumstances, I cried out suddenly and said sympathetically to my dear Lord:

"Oh, Master of the sea, speak your divine call again, that I may be like you, and cheer my broken soul," I said with a flood of tears.

And then I gratefully remembered I had previously begun succeeding wondrously in my high spiritual life; bonding with my nine-year-old son, instantly falling in love with my graceful and tidy wife, and working faithfully at my current job.

Far From Sight:

("The Adventures of Mister Big Tom")

But all at once, I felt incredibly small and very lonesome in that dark bobbing sea inside the beast belly with nowhere to get away. Yelling furiously in a burning rage and dwelling there with a wickedness of every terrible kind:

"I cannot escape."

Exasperatingly, I cried out into the deepening darkness, "Let go of me; you vicious brute!"

I said fiercely, in a blubbering tone. The flowing water was all around me. At that fearful time, I thought offensively, 'Now I must go where the Lord cannot see me.' But I steadfastly continued looking eagerly to him for needed help.

"Oh, my God, my God," I wailed, please help me, Lord! "Where are you?"

"Oh, please, let me out!"

"I continued begging God for mercy and yelling to the great heavenly sky!

"Lord, Lord! Remember me!

Have mercy on me, my Lord," I said vehemently.

Sheer terror was gripping my soul, and my whole life was passing before my eyes.

"And I shouted again."

"Lord, Lord! Remember me! Have mercy on me, my Lord!"

While I am shocked by the trials, along with hardships and other complimentary extreme worries, surprisingly one of my old girlfriends (a vivacious redbone with a cynical sense of humor) argues that we are happy where we are and that we should be grateful for the time we have together.

Then The Unthinkable Happened:

Only just as I finally realize the value of my alternative life. I see the responsible gunman for the third time, he said, "Tuff, who is now a brilliant friend." He's a passionate, fully devoted follower of Jesus Christ with an inspiring testimony to God's faithfulness. And ask him to help me go back to my past life; for instance, my alternative life is religiously based on a dreadful misinterpretation. But vulnerable, while being sorrowful about my fearful situation, "Tuff politely informs me that there is nothing he can do."

So, my personal epiphany jolts me back to my former life. On one (surprisingly) hot summer day in late June, along with the fiery sun glaring down upon me from above. In minor addition to my jolly living in that notable town in New Castle, to my dear family, with my devoted wife and brilliant son. Until lively now as I presently realize, isolated and unfulfilled alternative life, on a gloomy and unpleasant summer day.

"My vulnerable soul gave up all hope, but then I instantly remembered the Lord."

The Main Character Talks Continue:

A Miracle beyond Belief:

In economic desperation, I run back to God. And humbly beg to be allowed to live my former life again.

I understand correctly my sacred calling was simply to feed and faithful shepherd God's dear people with his divine word. Then I rolled about in the prominent belly and cried all along. I knowingly lay in the mythical beast of private hell in a little heap, like thrown—away garbage. Unbearable pain gripped my dear brown soul.

Then I cried fiercely unto the Lord and said thoughtfully:

"I pray unto thee, O Lord, I pray to thee, please forgive me—for the mortal sins I have committed against thee, and the sins I cannot naturally see."

"I pray unto thee, O Merciful God, I pray to thee, please forgive and forget all my sins, for Jesus' Holy name I do humbly pray. And now I'm sorry, Lord. And next time I'll faithfully obey."

I said in a breathy voice of entreaty. After that, I willingly let out the fierce breath I hadn't realized I was holding.

Victory at Sea:

Suddenly, after swimming very hard for three miserable days and three terrible nights, my humbly prayer is answered in the final moments:

"All of a sudden, I am no longer that defiant and uncooperative guy, my heart is changed. After all, the spirit of my soul which was passing away from under me clung to my triumph, convinced of my victory from the devil's belly and hell's jaws."

And at that time, immediately the mighty, massive beast came alongside to New Castle Town and rested peacefully on the white and glare-looking sand. It gave a little shudder as its prominent jaws were far and wide open. And I gracefully came a strolling forth out upon its mighty tongue on the grassy shore of my dazzling big brown soul.

Right away! God repeated impressively his supreme order:

"You will be my divine prophet. So go and preach the glorious gospel to all the dear people of New Castle Town this day," the Lord said in a gentle but firm voice.

By the way, the command to go is sometimes harder than the command to stay. Many people do not want to pull up stakes and move on, for commitment is costly. It is easier to simply stay and hang about. There are many "lollygag" Christians with their nose stuck doggedly in a Bible. They barely look up. They fiercely opposed the dear Lord. And steadfastly refused to obey his divine commandments. They typically did what they naturally wanted to do.

Mister Big Tom's Obedience:

("A Man of Honor and Virtue")

Certainly, Mister Big Tom faithfully kept his fulfilled promise. He earnestly warned the precious people of New Castle Town that the dear Lord was angry with their evil ways. And because they had seen him step out of the huge fanged mouth of (as a book of my innocent childhood wisely put it,) 'the whole big fish,' they sincerely believed what he said and did as the Lord commanded.

Then Mister Big Tom rose and said, "God is merciful unto us." He explains that mercy is connected to God's faithfulness towards us and that: "When one feels the mercy of God, he feels a great shame for himself and for his sin."

However, thankfully, Mister Big Tom freely, willingly, cheerfully, and carefully obeyed the holy call of God with the same faith and confidence that guided the Prophet Jonah. Therefore, he is tremendously excited about being safe once again on the relatively cool dry ground. Upon which he run home joyously, where his lovely wife and little son are waiting eagerly to receive him.

"But quite honestly, I think that I am undoubtedly the lucky one," said thoughtfully him.

"That the imminent danger on the raging water is surely over and I'm home at completed last."

Surprisingly, Liaduia came back upstairs to our chic bedroom, while I was sleeping soundly. "Hello," she shouted in a craggy voice. "Wake up, Mister Big Tom, wake up!"

"Why are you still sleeping? Your breakfast is ready!"

I answer gently in a muffled voice, "Okay, coming dear."

With my head tucked underneath the glossy cover. When I finally woke up; I was like, whoa, what happened? That wasn't a terrible dream that was just like one of those like life-altering experiences. I was trapped inside the prominent belly of a large, gigantic whale and it seemed like it was forever.

"I mean . . . I would never disobey God again, after that," I said gently in a terrible, silence voice. My shapely head is pounding like a sledgehammer has been pounding furiously my brain.

And then shortly after that, I realized, "Hey, God's Spirit instantly fills me up and lives peacefully in my dear heart." And with a wide sultry summer smile upon my gentle face. "I humbly thank God for properly filling me with his Holy Spirit and carefully directing my beloved soul," said thoughtfully Mister Big Tom; as he was sitting comfortably on the leading edge of his oak chair; at the loaded table having breakfast with his charming wife, lovely Mrs. Liaduia and his dear son, Little Tom.

Narrator Talks:

ALIVE, I CRIED FIERCELY

The Ultimate Saga of Mister Big, Big Tom:

In his desperate journey to obeying God, experiencing Him, and finally allowing Him to take over the control of his disobedient life, Thomas Blueberry has gratefully accepted God's divine call to preach the gospel unto them. Along with his careless submissions, his shapely head, his stubby, and somewhat ridiculous beard, he speaks the teachings of the Lord Jesus Christ from the Holy Bible. And now his faithful soul willingly preaches the good news of the Kingdom of God to all the dear people of New Castle Town.

"I'm sure God must be a blessed comfort to him."

The story of the fugitive Mister Big Tom swallowed up by a whale (in whose prominent belly he spends three days and three nights). Therefore, a fierce glance sincerely convinced him he was watching his soul float in a boundless sea of God's gracious favor and undeserved love that never quits.

Temporarily, Thomas Blueberry rode inside of a whale's high-flying belly; battling fiercely every obstacle and cherishing the profound silence of every moment, before discovering the purpose of his (as he now knows) divine calling.

The journey brought him through the notorious town of New Castle. And across the deep blue seas, where he discovered a wider range of real people with the same sense of purpose: "To let go (of his selfishness)—and let God (manifest His will in him)."

While floating towards the terror of this classic story, Thomas Blueberry suddenly concludes that his life outlook completely changed after his Jonah experience. In his mind, something clicks, and in his surprise, he seems to have a different view about his faith and fear. With this perspective, then, it seems after taking into consideration the attitude or mood of a poor rebellious soul (for example, fear, guilt, shame, etc.) is a miserable tormented soul if it's not dealt with properly.

As a direct result of which, his philosophical perspective was always to carefully compare what he undoubtedly saw to what he knew before. As a jolly, long-married man who was near death on the undefeated run from God. Mister Big Tom regrettably chose a selfish path and now he must suffer horribly. He swims aimlessly about the watery doom of New Castle Town. In the visible vein of a sultry summer day in late June, which the distant sun slowly floats nearby. And the great mammal takes him down into the gloomy deep-sea of the mighty soul. Along with rare bits of soaked seaweed and his glossy brown skin carefully covered with bubbling-bleached scalps. And from the sizzling light of a lurking beast that was swallowing him up. He went down; down into the smoldering heat, which the fiery sunset gilded around him. And he was in trouble, deep trouble, he called to the dear Lord for divine help, and He answered him. From the dark below, the dear Lord listened at his eager voice, and his cry for urgent help before the Lord came instantly into his visible ears.

Soon, however, after a long silence, the dear Lord said:

"Why do you call me, 'Lord', and do not obey what I tell you?"

Then he looked at the Lord, his God (with a sad and serious gesture raised his arms,) and answered, "But you, a Lord, how long shall I suffer? Lord, please," I beg! Help! Help! "Oh help me, Lord," again he called.

His fear is on, as he moved by divine grace through the creepy, slimy substance that naturally shrunk from his lively touch; around and about, up and down repeatedly; he cannot calm down. It is him he wants to show that his thoughts are wrong. The people of New Castle Town should care for everyone and everything that God has made.

Just like the Flying Dutchman (refers to the captain of the lost ship, the captain, Cornelius Vanderdecken), Mister Big Tom is doomed to sail the seas in a monster's belly until he is redeemed by God. He's a model prisoner of his own fears. Mister Big Tom experienced that having overwhelmingly rejected the glorious gospel (to work God's vineyard), he had merely increased his moral responsibility for his own actions. He instantly rejected the spiritual life humbly offered to him. And was guilty of self-murder; he naturally had no one to reasonably blame.

"His radical blood was admittedly upon his own dirty hand."

Perhaps, he naturally felt the historic force of those breathtaking words which the dear Lord prophetically spoke to Ezekiel (in chapter 33 and verse 8); his divine punishment would come directly from God. If he typically failed to faithfully report to the dear people the angelic messages God divinely gave him.

That's why, in one swift movement. He was eagerly snatched and swallowed up by a monstrous beast that is doomed to sail the oceans in search of freedom and peace. His fierce cries for needed help go unanswered, and suddenly he instantly disappears into the deep-sea.

While he was gently in the ample stomach of the noble beast for three miserable days and three sleepless nights, he sincerely prayed to the dear Lord, his God, and He heard him. From out of the prominent belly of eternal hell pleaded bitterly him.

"Please, God, let me out," Mister Big Tom begged.

He was trembling down to the top of his toes, to the shallow bottom of his bubbling-blistered feet. Typically surrounded by slippery rocks and polished pebbles, with one quiet toe in front of the other, they are racing along in the mighty ocean floor.

As a logical consequence of his running away from God and alive now, he's running eagerly to the dear Lord:

"He was in total shock! You can tell from the comprehensive look on his fierce face that this was no joke!" cried the Narrator.

"Hum!"

"Being in the belly of a whale is no joke," scarcely said Mister Big Tom, strolling forth out upon its mighty tongue.

I mean, "No joke!"

The people's eyes widened, and they mumbled, "What terrible thing did you do against your God?"

CHAPTER 1

DISOBEDIENCE: "THE YOUNG FUGITIVE"

GOD CALLS, MISTER BIG TOM — WILLFULLY DISOBEYS:

Breaking God's Law

(What Mister Big Tom did—willfully disobeying or Breaking God's Law—Is Sin)

Narrator Talks (Via the Leading Protagonist)**:**

I remember (not so very long ago) in the glowing light of a mid-summer day in late June; along with the fiery sun glaring down upon him from above. Therefore, repeatedly, the humble narrator politely narrates the heroic story of the most significant character.

I equally know Thomas Blueberry as Mister Big Tom, one of the leading industries, most influential executives. He has been passionate about helping people find themselves but instantly balks at God's direct call. Although I am balky, I'm a very tractable and happy guy, living peacefully the high spirit life in New Castle Town with my wonderful family: my beautiful, sweet, loving wife, Mrs. Liaduia and the most lovable little boy in the world, my dear son Little Tom; for I am my family's life as fully as they are mine.

For a moment Mister Big Tom sat quietly (leaning forward in his hard-backed chair) while the grieving dad made small talk and puttered around wondering if God is actually good. As the noon hour approached, and after a few seconds of more companionable support, Mister Big Tom said:

TOMMY R. BANKS, SR.

This is undoubtedly a sad day for me. It pains me to see my old pal (Mr. Jed Reston), who has meant so much to me, on the grassy verge of giving up.

Man's Need of Salvation:

Mister Big Tom Talks:

"I am breaking for a delightful lunch and thirsty now."
Mister Big Tom said shortly after consoling a much-loved father shattered by an unbelievable loss of his only son. He was murdered in a senseless shooting outside a New Castle local shopping center on Thursday night. And why dear Mr. Jed desperately needs personal salvation from the Lord Jesus Christ. Oft-times, however, the concept of eternal life has little or no meaning for him.

Meanwhile, I was at my gentle office—busy—working my butt off on Father's Day weekend. I am trying intentionally to calm a sad, broken-hearted, sincerely crying bitterly pessimistic father. And I continued leaning forward in my hard-backed chair and looking sympathetically into his despairing—eyes:

"Oh, I'm sorry for your loss," I said, speaking in a slow and gentle voice.

I kindly continue telling the newly bereaved dad (less than a day) that salvation is God's way of dealing with evil; and providing a means for you to receive eternal life in fellowship with Him.

Therefore, salvation comes only just by God's grace and through Jesus Christ when a person accepts Him as Lord and Savior.

"Well, Mr. Jed," Mister Big Tom said, "Do you want to believe on Him?"

"Who is him, anyhow, a friend?"

"Yes, the Lord God Almighty (more of a Yahweh of a guy)," I wisely said to dear Mr. Jed.

He gently shook his head with a wistful sadness.

"Oh, I do, I do. In fact—"

I Want To Believe:

"What must I do?" Mr. Jed (the bewailed father) said wistfully in that weak voice.

"Personal faith in Christ is the logical answer," I said promptly in a soft, compassionate voice. After that I instantly began reciting by joyful heart a remarkable passage of sacred Scripture. And politely told him that Jesus says to you—me:

"I am the way, and the truth, and the life; no one comes to the Father, but through me— John 14:6; (KJV)."

His frail voice faltered as he asked anxiously, "What does personal faith mean?"

The Holy Bible teaches that personal faith affirms that "you have been crucified with Christ. It is no longer you who live, but Christ who lives in you."

"Repentance and faith are indissoluble experiences of grace. Repentance is a genuine turning from evil toward God, and faith is the acceptance of Jesus Christ and commitment of the entire personality to Him as Lord and Savior.

"Finally, Mr. Jed, you should be baptized in obedience to Jesus Christ and as a testimony to your faith," in the same gentle but clear voice I said.

After three hours and fifty-eight minutes of consoling the mournful colleague, then the father told me that 'he could not go on; that he misses his son very much! And that he doesn't know how to go on without him in his life,' the boy's father, a disheartening old age man, very vulnerable and dismayed, bundled up in a long loose overcoat against the warm June day. His eyes dripped continuously with tears. He was merely on the critical point of giving up.

"So like many of those inside the quite office, I said I am here for you and remember God's eternal salvation gives us the divine strength to carry on."

"Wouldn't you like some coffee?" I urged him.

"I don't want anything. I'm all right now, Mister Big Tom, thanks!" he said with an expressive smile.

"Then, all of a sudden, I felt very cagey," "Then, all of a sudden, there is something strange started happening," "And then, suddenly, there's something popped into my head that just will not let me be." In a quiet and inaudible voice:

"I instantly thought to preach the gospel surely was not for me," Mister Big Tom said thoughtfully.

Therefore, my sense of immediacy within each thing that happens to me also leads to my sense of contumacy. Because I experience my further temporally, with the present moment becoming a part of my past, I view my life as being in a state of persistent refusal. And like the Prophet Jonah's Story, I said what I thought most reasonable people would say:

I did not want to be a prophet, so I pushed it away.

"I tried to forget what I heard, ignore it, and go on with my dear life."

Unfortunately, this approach doesn't work any better for me than it did for the Prophet Jonah, and my life quickly unravels.

The Main Character Balks at God's Call:

Mister Big Tom and Tuff Talks:

I mean morally, it was precisely a beautiful, sultry summer day and shortly after I started walking through the narrow footpath beside the Old Little Road. It quite surprised me to hear the gentle voice of God from eternal heaven, politely calling me by my official name.

"But Lord?" "I'm here. What do you want?" I answered, looking all around to see where the voice came from.

And God said to me, "Surrender, Mister Big Tom, it's useless to resist."

"You will be my inspired prophet this lovely day. Therefore, I want you to preach the glorious gospel to all the dear people of New Castle Town. I have heard about the many evil things the people are doing there. So go now and tell them to stop doing such evil things," the Lord said in a still small but authoritative voice.

"It horrified me." The only thing I knew about prophets, was what I had heard in Sunday-school and Bible-study: prophets were weird, dressed in animal skins and always shouting about the coming destruction. "But there's no way I will go," I said quietly, almost inaudibly, as I justly feared to do as God commanded.

"I will run, run, and run; which means I'll stay so far away from the Lord's divine presence."

It is at the end of my encounter with God (after God spoke). I was, however, afraid to surrender completely to the Holy Spirit, so I kept controlling myself. I did not wish to preach to the people of New Castle Town, for they continue to be the wicked enemies of God.

The dear people lived within the sinful city (noted for its large magnificent buildings, with tall solid walls) and were happy to stay there. Just as long as they can do whatever they want. And there will not be any consequences for their willful disobedience of that which God's word declares as foolishness.

In the meantime, however, I am intentionally walking (here and there) alone the narrow path. While gently lowering my shapely head and reminiscing kindly a personal bit about the authoritative voice I had undoubtedly heard; and so, after a few breathless seconds of more gloomy thoughts and more of my rebellious ways.

First Encounter with Bad Guy:

Then suddenly, I walk into a local convenience store, where a dirty mean man, unknown, rudely barges in screaming at us. The man said bluntly, "Give me all your money, or I will kill y'all!"

"Are you sure you want to do this?" Mister Big Tom asked.

"This isn't a nice thing to do to anybody. I mean?"

"You be quiet," the robber interrupted, "It's a stick-up! Put your hands up!! And give me all your money, now!! That's right, give me all you got!" he said in a loud voice.

The store clerk believes that the man is joking and refuses to give him the money.

The Judas Gun:

(".38 Special")

The furious man pulls out a small loaded handgun from his pocket and is about to shoot the clerk and me. He was shouting at us with such force and intensity. It was like having a space heater blowing directly in our faces.

He shouted over and over and very loudly.

"I'm going to kill y'all," he shouted. Somebody going to die up in here today, if you don't do what I say:

"Put your hands up! And give me all your money, now! That's right, give me all you got!" he said in a nasty harsh tone, and certainly, it surprised us very much.

Twist of Faith:

I jumped like I'd already been shot with my hands hoisted in the sultry air. The store clerk didn't put up her hands when the gunman said:

"Put your hands up." Instead, she turned to me, and asked, "What does he want!" I thought the gun should have given her a clue. And then I turned to the store clerk, and politely offered to help her by defusing the situation quickly:

"I asked the gunman his name??"

"And do you love God??"

"In an attempt to calm him," Mister Big Tom said in a peaceful voice.

"My name is Tuff!" the gunman says in a forceful mood.

"So—get back—I want nothing to do with God!!"

"Okay, that's your choice." But Tuff, "you must realize that your only hope is God through the precious blood of Jesus Christ, and the power of his Holy Spirit," Mister Big Tom said.

He looked at me with feigned surprise.

"Who are you?? You're crazy!! I don't know what you're talking about!!" he says in a very exciting and undermines way.

"Tuff, you know God is calling you in some way," Mister Big Tom says in a calm voice.

Oh, while we're on the subject—yeah, I have a divine message for you from God, through the miraculous power of his Holy Spirit. God sincerely wants to lead you to the good things he has in store for you."

A Compunctious Reaction:

Tuff—quotes: "A message from God???" he says, raising an eyebrow, and feeling a stab of guilt at his own horrible acts.

But, he with a chuckle replied. "That sounds really interesting, okay, let's hear it," he said as he aimed his pistol carefully at me.

I politely told the villainous thief that, of course, my God is the God of eternal heaven. And there was the look of the penitent man in his eyes. He looked at me sadly with a passionate tear, and then I told him, that he needs to make up his peace with God.

"Make peace with God?" he said, running a trembling hand across his cheek, "Why—so!!" He went a step nearer and asked, "Why do I need to make up my peace with God or ask forgiveness if I don't want anything to do with God??" asked wonderingly, Tuff.

"Because it is necessary you should regain the grace of God which you have lost gracefully by your yielding to sin, and which He is the source of all your happiness."

"Therefore, the everlasting mercy of God may intentionally withhold us or gently ease our expected punishment," Mister Big Tom said politely in a prophesying way.

Narrator Talks (Via the Main Character, a. k. a. Mister Big Tom)**:**

Finally, after a long and uncomfortable silence, he said with quiet intensity, making eye contact, and his choice of sacred words came as a divine revelation from his recent past and his distant future. His gentle voice hardened as he spoke more rapidly using a simple mantra:

"Tuff, come now, don't waste any more time! Stop here and don't be a thief that winds up in Hell! You must follow Yahweh and do whatever He tells you!!"

Unsurprisingly, Mister Big Tom uttered, as he allegedly won the would-be robber with a persuasive word from God.

Wow, The Odds Shift Radically:

The tables turn dramatically as Tuff quietly puts his loaded Judas gun away. I kindly led him around inside the big store for a few consistent minutes, then opened one of the ornate doors and gently took him outside. I briefly continue sharing in common the fundamental teachings of Jesus Christ with him (having a heart-to-heart talk). Mister Big Tom's divine message was simple as a cold slap in Tuff's passionless face.

The Perfect Plan:

However, I politely explained that eternal redemption and eternal salvation is God's way of saving people from their terrible sin and its unavoidable consequence (eternal death); carefully making you and me better for his intended purpose (eternal God's inspired Word).

The words which commence Romans 3:24,

"Being justified freely by his grace through the redemption that is in Christ Jesus —(KJV)."

Sincerely meaning what Christ did for us at Calvary that He willingly died on the Cross in your lovely place and mine. He died a sinner's death and was buried in a sinner's grave, but rose with all power in his mighty hands.

"Tuff the only way a person can be born again is to believe in Jesus Christ as their Lord and Savior."

The infallible Word says thoughtfully,

> *"For God so loved the world, that he gave his only begotten Son, that whosoever believeth in him should not perish, but have everlasting life — John 3:16; (KJV)."*

He paused.

"Oh, this presents the God kind of brotherly love (agape)," he said, directly.

"But it is perfect. You can trust God with your shortcomings," he smiled firmly.

(And so, Tuff, John 3:16 not only talks about *the magnitude of God's love,* but it also speaks about *the fairness of God's love.*)

God Is Fair

(In Mercy, Grace, and Favor):

"So, what God has done for others, He can and will do the same for you. Just ask Him and believe. He already knows your needs. God is looking for people that will put their trust in Him. He is there to give you what you need."

"Therefore, the plan is simple. God says that you are His divine creation and that He loves you very much. He says you can be saved today, even this very precious moment, if you believe in Him and ask Him to save you?"

"Oh, wow that would be cool to do!" "And hmm, "How can I do that?" Tuff asked me.

"Well, first, you must realize you are a sinner, and your only hope is Christ."

"Do you know' what God says about us?"

"No, tell me, please—I have no idea," Tuff said wonderingly. "No idea at all."

Well, the Lord wisely said:

> *"For all have sinned, and come short of the glory of God —Romans 3:23; (KJV)."*

"Surely, you know that we have done wrong things which God say is a sin."

Therefore, Tuff as a sinner, you understand that it separates you from God; your sins have hidden God's face from you, because the Lord is holy, harmless, and undefiled.

The word of God says your sin separates you from God and condemns you to die apart from Him because you do not believe and receive His forgiveness.

Also, God tells us in the wonderful book of Romans (and throughout the well-worn Holy Bible) that,

> "The wages of sin is death; but the gift of God is eternal life through Jesus Christ our Lord—Romans 6:23; (KJV)."

"Sadly, Tuff this includes eternal separation from God and everlasting punishment in hell."

"Yes, perhaps you are right Mister Big Tom. Besides, God wants me to pray and to change my old ways to become the righteousness of Him."

"Of course God does!" Mister Big Tom said sympathetically.

Also, the following Scripture wisely says:

> "If my people, which are called by my name, shall humble themselves, and pray, and seek my face, and turn from their wicked ways; then will I hear from heaven, and will forgive their sin, and will heal their land—2 Chronicles 7:14; (KJV)."

Indeed, I continue speaking gently to him the Lord's divine Words,

> "Forasmuch as you know that you were not redeemed with corruptible things, as silver and gold, from your vain conversation received by tradition from your fathers; but with the precious blood of Christ, as of a lamb without blemish and without spot
> —1 Peter 1:18, 19; (KJV)."

Tuff Talks:

"I must humbly confess, I'm admittedly an awful person," Tuff said, unfortunately.

"But now I understand how to relate to God. Thank you, Mister Big Tom, I received my divine prophecy today and it was wonderful. The prophesied word was accurate and right on time."

"This prophetic word from the Lord; it was truly a word of encouragement, direction, and promise. Thank you is not enough. Only the Lord knew what you revealed to me."

A Matter of Faith:

"Before, I wasn't very strong in my belief," Tuff said sympathetically. With this new view of God, the Bible started to make sense to him.

"So it's a good start, right??"

Mister Big Tom Talks:

"Yes, yes, of course it is!"

And faith (sincere faith) is something you must have right from the humble start, before taking off!"

It is for the dear sake of divine salvation, Tuff willingly surrendered his loaded Judas gun; just before taking off in the cobblestone streets of New Castle Town. And now, he's a whole new person; a jolly man blessed by God's eternal truth. And it's because God changed him. I could see it in him. I could sense it. Tuff had finally made his way to the God who loved him and had never stopped pursuing him.

Amazingly, Tuff more thoroughly believes Jesus remains undoubtedly his faithful Lord. In time, he sufficiently learns to recognize God and works towards to live peacefully with Him.

It is in fact, quite the exact opposite of what Tuff at likely first believed. In the middle of his wicked life; for a rare instance, Tuff naturally thought his destructive behavior was truly a divine blessing of God, but now he sincerely believes this is not really a spiritual gift. Instead, it's more of a terrible curse than a mighty miracle, because he had sinned significantly and fell short of the dear Lord's everlasting glory.

Since then, Tuff has willingly accepted God's divine gift of eternal salvation through the wonderful preaching of the Holy Spirit. All the same, eternal salvation comes only from God's divine plan; His grace and through His Son, when a person accepts Jesus Christ as Lord and Savior. He instantly becomes a whole unfamiliar person.

Moreover, a changed man (because of an encounter with God) through the Spirit that is in him. The inspired word transformed in Tuff's moved heart, that thief turned from evil to good, or at least into a more Christ-like character.

I politely offered to help Tuff before taking a delightful lunch and going to sleep in my cozy upper-story Castle house bedroom; accessible by the cool, breezy conditioning air; with an antique mushroom staircase; featured cypress-wood construction and a bluish-white moon roof; with its picture walls (upon which was very full) and elegantly furnished with a new soft-cane Rattan sofa.

Therefore, gently, I looped my bulky arms around my lovely wife and beloved son and sincerely held them as my dear life fades instantly into the radiant days of yore.

In time, my moral vision instantly dims. In all that remains are the many fond memories; I have come to know, not in my conscious mind, but in my rosy flesh. It is undoubtedly just my moral imagination, that ability to think of being true to God that needs to be activated.

Subconsciously, however, when a hasty glance at our own lives. It credibly threatens to make us uncomfortable, and we often look at ourselves for some moral good deed to put our conscious mind at ease. But then, on a certain day of which I could never think without a quicker beating of the dear heart. I instantly thought, and through my stunning disquietedness passed out of a beautiful summer day, into a dark and dreadful sleepless night.

CHAPTER 2

A DECADE OF SIN

MISTER BIG TOM'S
BLAST FROM THE PAST, UNEXPECTEDLY:

Ten Years Before — Through Hell In High Water

(By the Spirit of God He Perish, And By the Breath of His Nostrils Are He Consumed)

Mister Big Tom and Tuff Talks:

(I was twenty-seven.) The foggy night is over, and the following morning it's a dark and gloomy summer day. I wake up traumatized inside the smoldering belly of a mighty, sightless beast with an oversized monster's flowing tail, which proves both wise and gentle. And with deepening gloom and visible smoke and with hideous noises that sound like someone crying in a horrible way. And then, for the breathless instant out of the prominent belly of a burning hell, "Alive, I cried fiercely," fighting to get out.

It's Humid and Embarrassing:

I am also unmarried and living with personal regret outside the noble city (It's extremely boiling and unpleasant) in an uncomfortably narrow and muddy-looking two-story shotgun house; accessible by the dry, sultry desert air, with a deteriorating staircase; featured cedar-wood construction and a bluish-white metal roof, with its blank walls ivy-sand (upon which was very bare), and was merely furnished with an old beat-up pale-brown Naugahyde wood sofa.

"I'm afraid," I said timidly.

"I'm really, really hot in this shotgun house; filled with creepy, slimy substance that shrunk (like squishy walls sagging) from my lively touch."

"I'm falling apart."

"I'm barely breathing."

Although I am all along with my big and bulky Bible: a thick, quarto-sized stacked book with a black back and a leather cover. Its well-worn pages were rough and craggy. And I don't know what to do in ninety-five soundless feet of murky water. While being separated from the forgotten rest of the dear world as continuous daylight shattered away.

Mister Big Tom Seems A Bit Discombobulated:

Mister Big Tom Talks Continue:

Feeling genuinely shocked and terribly confused, I rushed back to work in New Castle Town, but no one supposedly knows me; not even the store clerk, or nor do my closest friends gratefully recognize me.

The Good-Hearted Bad Man:

Confused, I run desperately to the cobbled street and encounter the affirmed gunman, Tuff. He is now a born-again Christian with a dark baleful past, Tuff is indeed a former hired gun, the most lethal Southerner assassin ever created. After decades of violent work, the dear Lord, he says graciously with his eager hands in the sultry air like a Pentecostal praising God; who had blessed him with spiritual joy and lasting peace; who has miraculously delivered him from indescribably evil, especially when He faithfully redeemed Tuff from mortal sin and all kinds of portentous crimes?

Miracles around Us:

Narrator Talks (Via Tuff)**:**

"God continues faithfully to work in unexpected ways to divinely reveal Himself to us. I am exceedingly thankful that God has graciously led me to a saving faith in Christ."

Tuff staggered not at God's precious gift through unbelief but was strong in steadfast faith; giving all praise, honor, and divine glory to God.

"Jesus Christ is my Lord and dear Saviour. I sincerely love him very much. I earnestly want to go to eternal heaven when I die, to be with Jesus," Tuff added wistfully. Therefore, he gently continued sharing his precious testimonies of divine miracles, miraculous healings, and other inspirational stories.

Tuff Talks:

"Mister Big Tom, it might seem hard to actually believe but I went to jail for almost a year. Before I met you and I never want to go back. A few days after I had left you, I got my old job back, and for a second time I was back on track."

"Just after that, I started getting very weak on my legs and later realized that I was not quite my normal self. Eventually, I had to sit down as the weakness in my legs got stronger and stronger. After that, it spread to the rest of my body. The feeling I had is best described as being completely sore."

"Carefully following a brief examination, the local doctors politely informed me I was paralyzed from the ample waist."

Unshakable Faith:

Tuff Talks Continue:

"To my pleasant surprise, I begin desperately to shed tears, refer to a sacred scripture and pray persistently," cried Tuff.

> *"Have mercy upon me, O Lord, for I am weak; O Lord, heal me; for my bones are troubled—Psalm 6:2; (KJV)."*

> *"Be gracious to me, O Lord, my heavenly Father of sufficient grace, everlasting mercy, and eternal peace; I come before you this sorrowful day. I sincerely believe in You, O Lord the Father almighty, Merciful God."*

> *"Heal me in the way that only you can; thank You, O God the Father of my Lord and Savior Jesus Christ; the one who faithfully delivers me from sin. Forgive me, and pour out your mercy upon me."*

> *"Praise be to You, O Lord Most High; my loving Father. In Jesus' name I make this request. Amen."*

And immediately my shapely legs made sturdy, and I glorified the God of my dear soul. Therefore, praise be to Yahweh, hallelujah! Wow, through my sincere beliefs and humble prayers, I'm miraculously healed by the divine power of the Lord Jesus Christ.

Yes, whoever is persistent (sufficient evidence of an unshakable faith) will gratefully receive:

> *"If you are persistent in humbly asking, God will willingly give to you.*
>
> *If you are persistent in diligently seeking, you will undoubtedly find.*
>
> *If you are persistent in knocking, the everlasting door will open for you."*

Then, all at once, Tuff said to Mister Big Tom, "God healed my paralyzed body." That is where I learned that God's healing power is not always instantaneous, but sometimes a creative process that takes time.

"Oh, wow, that's right!" Mister Big Tom said smilingly.

Then, God instantly reminded me of a prime example from the well-worn Holy Bible where Jesus willingly declared:

"They shall take up serpents; and if they drink any deadly thing, it shall not hurt them; they shall lay hands on the sick, and they shall recover— Mark 16:18; (KJV)."

"Soon after being completely healed I was very excited about God's healing power and told everybody I came in contact with," said thankfully Tuff, in his emotional way.

"Wow! This is unbelievable, Mister Big Tom said with excitement and surprise in his voice."

"I mean, unbelievable!" Mister Big Tom said at a loss for more words.

Victory in Grace:

"Needless to say, God miraculously saved me from violent crimes and criminal corruption! Although I was not saved at the likely time, I intentionally tried robbing you and the store clerk at gunpoint. Until now, I have been admittedly an awful person," Tuff cried inwardly. "I have knowingly committed unspeakable crimes and have done intentionally bad terrible things, but God has miraculously saved me."

Tuff Talks (Continue Via Narrator):

Meantime, Tuff faithfully continues relating the inspirational story of God's divine grace and his own salvation to Mister Big Tom. In a completely unbelievable episode; Tuff talks about a remarkable account of divine miracles, miraculous blessings, and life inside the private world of New Castle Town.

Upon of which he gently said: God, the Savior, has been good to me; but most of all when He faithfully delivered me from my terrible misfortunes. Therefore, you willingly see Mister Big Tom, when God tells you to go carefully in a certain direction; don't turn back. God's unmistakable way is always best. If you fully obey God and follow all his lovely commands, He will heartily rejoice in willingly doing you good. And (parenthetically) God will bless you at all precious times. "In everything you undoubtedly do," said thoughtfully Tuff, and he believed it; and that belief set his heart palpitating.

"Unsurprisingly, the Lord God will bless you just as He willingly promised you."

After that, Tuff, politely tell Mister Big Tom about how he suffered tremendously the horrific atrocity knowingly committed by arrested Thursday's local killer. Ironically, known as Old Blue, his former cellmate (He was naturally born in Big Foot, Arkansas, but moved to New Castle Town; where we grew up in foster homes.) We attended West Castle High School here in New Castle Town. Shortly before the promising start of my new faith life, Old Blue was in question for knowingly killing a young boy named Jack Reston ("He was the most sensible, quiet, clever young boy you would ever want to meet," Tuff told Mister Big Tom.)

Murder by Mistake:

("I Didn't Mean To Do It")

"Tuff said Old Blue was going to get in a fight with four bad guys. And his gun accidentally discharged, shooting Jack through the chest so that he afterward died."

Tuff also said he remember a young Jack Reston who didn't have many friends. Since his death, many junior boys have claimed that they have been Jack's friends. "I know for a fact that wasn't true," Tuff said.

Therefore, at a 10:05 p.m. press conference, high-ranking New Castle Police officials had leads, but didn't say whether old Blue had yet been identified as a possible suspect. When asked if he says why he voluntarily turned himself in, Old Blue said sympathetically, "He just wanted to do the right thing."

Graciously rendering to an arrest warrant affidavit, 41-year-old Blue called police at 8:55 p.m. Thursday night to turn himself in. They took him to the Department's Vehicle Crimes Unit, says the criminal affidavit; where he did "identify himself as the potential murderer. "That he willingly admitted that he did by mistake kill Jack, and he left the scene of a fatal crime," says solemnly the affidavit.

Mr. Blue took his gun inside the New Castle Town's Greenway Plaza, telling police it accidentally fired.

"Oh, I accidentally shot Jack in the chest."
"Why in God's name you do that??" the chief officer said.
"Well, I didn't mean to do it. It was an accident!"

Therefore, Tuff wraps up his rambling conversations with Mister Big Tom by telling him that Old Blue has a heavy dose of guilt to burden him. And while he regrets everything that happened; he wishes he can carefully undo his wrongs. I spoke with him sometimes, and he really feels disappointed.

Finally, Mister Big Tom spoke. His voice crackled (like a whip, full of heat and command), "But do you remember our conversation on that one dreadful day about late afternoon, some seventy-two hours ago?" Mr. Big Tom asked, looking at Tuff suspiciously.

"Yes, very well," Tuff said gratefully. You were right, God does love me.

"On top of that, God naturally wants us to have eternal joy and to become more like Him. "All the same, Mister Big Tom, sincerely thank you; for willingly sharing the Good News (i.e. the Gospel—nearly too precious good to be true news) of Jesus Christ with me. For instantly reminding me and gently encouraging my dear heart, over and over again. That it's all about the unconditional love of God, which is precisely in Jesus Christ our dear Lord."

"My fulfilled prophecy was so, so, so, so right on! Sincerely thank you, thank you, and thank you."

Tuff Talks Continue (Via the Narrator):

"In the meantime, Tuff carefully explains that Mister Big Tom is typically undergoing a traumatic experience, cloistered inside the prominent belly of an extremely large whale. He is constantly tormented in divine order to learn a lesson that is personal to Mister Big Tom's spiritual life. As a direct result, Tuff earnestly advises Mr. Big Tom to take the time to discover whatever it is that he dearly needs to naturally learn."

The Main Character Talks:

"Thanks, Tuff, I am overwhelmed with the word! Confirmation, confirmation, confirmation! The words you spoke to me have helped propel me to another dimension of God. Thank you so much!" Mister Big Tom said gratefully (holla at your boy).

Inside The Blueberry's Family:

Narrator Talks:

After a great deal of reasoning; and now, Thomas Blueberry instantly realizes he's single and living with personal regret the lively life that he definitely does not want to live. As a possible substitute, he is precisely a poor and destitute pawnshop salesman, who suffers greatly at the present time; only if he had not refused to willingly follow the dear Lord.

But nevertheless, he undoubtedly enjoys an exceptional family life (Which in fact, he misses very, very much!) Where he is an industrial executive of the NCT Industrial Direction, Incorporation; authorized retailer of industrial products including tools, hardware, fittings, valves, and materials. Thomas Blueberry's chosen profession has been faithfully related to active management and industrial relations. His peaceful job from the very beginning has been carefully helping dispirited people find themselves through positive thinking.

Though he has never acknowledged openly the divine call of God's Spirit, he has been influenced by the well-worn Holy Bible, God's Words and Scriptures. Which were available in English translation, especially those of the original Hebrews language like the Books of the Old and New Testament?

It is due to his biblical influences that Thomas Blueberry has been willingly helping people since his youth days. And it was said that he would preach in 1979 where he had witnessed the divine power of God's inspired Word in direct action through him.

He's been happily married for almost ten successful years this July. To his devoted wife, lovely Mrs. Liaduia, a fifth-grade school teacher at New Castle Elementary. Who specializes in modern mathematics? And naturally has one brilliant nine-year-old son he misses repeatedly!

ALIVE, I CRIED FIERCELY

Narrator and Mister Big Tom's Wife Talks (Mrs. Liaduia):

My Husband Is Missing:

A few hours later, disappointed Mrs. Liaduia learns that her dear husband has been abducted temporarily into a deep ocean of overflowing water, but not to be killed by drowning. Instead, he wakes up traumatized inside the prominent belly of a mighty, sightless beast with deepening gloom and smoke and with hideous noises!

"Oh! Oh, my goodness gracious!" she said regretfully in a dismayed voice.

After that, she fell silent for a good long time until she finally said, "My husband is gone." Mister Big Tom and I are getting ready to celebrate our tenth wedding anniversary in a couple of precious weeks. This is a significant achievement for any lovely couple, but for us, it is especially important. You instantly see, for the last three radiant days of our marriage Mr. Big Tom struggled mightily with his peaceful disobedience toward God, he refuses to willingly obey God's direct command. And he has fiercely rejected the dear Lord's humble calling on his precious life."

"Seventy-two countless hours ago I had my reasonable doubts that Mister Big Tom would even live to see our tenth anniversary. Let alone that he would be genuinely enjoying a good healthy marriage."

By the way, I finally did realize when my dear husband was running furiously from God's justly calling on his dear life. I was playing a part in my beloved husband's fierce determination to run from God. I had become vulnerable. And as a result, I was making it easier for my dear husband to undoubtedly continue running on his destructive path. It was only after I had shifted my own focus that positive changes began to take place.

Above and Beyond:

Meanwhile, for the past three radiant days and three sultry nights, I reasonably blamed every problem on Mister Big Tom and his disobedience to God. It was naturally an easy out. I was ignoring my own challenges and was instantly in passionate denial. While

Mister Big Tom was running away from the dear Lord, I could not because I was consumed with Mister Big Tom. My every conscious thought revolved around him:

> How long will he run?
> Why did my dear husband not want to preach the gospel?
> Why did my dear husband disobey God?
> Will my miserable husband get away with it?
> Why can't he just stop running?

For the past three radiant days and three sultry nights, I was living harmoniously a consistent cycle of arguing persuasively and crying, instantly putting myself into dangerous situations and feeling alone and confused. Every successful attempt that I naturally made to carefully help my dear husband seemed to fail spectacularly.

"Oh, well, I sincerely hope his dear life gets better and less cantankerous." He certainly must either find gentle grace or be forced to it," said wistfully dear Mrs. Liaduia at completed last; indeed, he must.

"Therefore, trust and obey Him, my dear love as your God and your Lord and Savior; pray if you can, we too are praying with you."

Big Moments Like Father, Like Son:

Narrator Talks:

Soon after that, Mister Big Tom's young son (Little Tom) a precocious but lovable, light brown color faced nine-year-old boy. He is mystified by his dear father's disappearance and naughty behavior towards God. Suddenly, Little Tom instantly realizes his father's divine secret, naturally thinks he is a removable alien but a friendly one. And voluntarily decide to help him in miraculously surviving his former life.

Mister Big Tom and Mrs. Liaduia's Young Son Talks (Little Tom):

"Mom, you okay?" the youngster asks, regarding his mother across the room, rushing to her side.

"Yes dear," she answered, wrapping her arms around him and holding on; with a sunny smile through her tears, coming like a rainbow. "Then she looked around at him, and told him to never forget that your father loves you!"

"Yes ma'am," Little Tom said, and tears ran down his cheeks.

Amazingly, not too long ago, "I thought my dad was an alien-human being; whose life was going downhill before my very eyes." Concerned I rushed towards the figure, shivering—and when it was about a short distance away from me—I saw a young, short-haired man—dressed in a long black coat. Then the man passed before my face and made the hair on my head stand up on end. His face, neck, and hands were scarred with blistering-bleached spots.

"Unfortunately, in bed at home, I could not sleep for all the buzzing of zeroes and ones in my head. I noticed he started being distance—and then he vanished as I reached out to him—and told him goodbye—and that I loved him."

"I was so upset because he's all I got—and a few days after that he came to me—crouching on one knee—and broke down."

"I venture, then to ask, what were the consequences of your decision?"

Mister Big Tom's Confessions:

"Why I ran," Dad said, looking away for a moment, avoiding my question.

"Yes, he told me about everything."

"He told me about the first time God called him, and why he refused."

"He told me that he really believes God wants him sharing how needless pain it has caused him (and others around him). God placed on dad's heart to come and follow Him several days ago, but he refused Him. He wanted his right to do as he pleased," Little Tom quotes.

"So, back to our earlier question—what were the consequences of your decision?" Little Tom asks.

"Oh God, the last two days of my life have been miserable, and everything I tried to do turned out to be a mess and pretty much a failure."

"I basically fell away from God once I decided to run my life without including God in it."

"Oh, I still prayed but only when I was near complete despair and needed help," Mister Big Tom said worriedly and most of my answers then were, "No."

"What did you run away for, Daddy??" he asked.

The answer is very simple:

"Because I was not living as God called me to. I wanted to live my life my way," Mister Big Tom says as he was trembling with fear.

Little Toom Talks Continue:

"In the meantime, Dad continues his explanations and finally, he explained to me, all of his struggles, dwelling in that dark prison cell inside the fish belly, and how he tried to go forward with God's command," Little Tom said, in a voice that was—certainly, very calm indeed.

Narrator Talks:

Nonetheless, how could such a well-off man drift away from his heavenly calling and fall into disobedience? It begins with a partial, incomplete knowledge of God's character.

Thomas Blueberry was given a powerful revelation of God's grace and mercy. He testified of God's graciousness. He was given the same revelation Jonah received when the Lord called him to preach judgment to the city-nation Nineveh. But instead of warning Nineveh, Jonah fled.

So, why did Mister Big Tom run? Why did he refuse to obey God's clearly revealed command? We know he was a man of God's Word. After all, the Lord speaks clearly to those who commune with Him. And God doesn't choose His, servants, carelessly. Evidently, He saw something in Mister Big Tom. However, it is possible that the dear Lord chose this sensible man because of his precious gifts: A persuasive voice or a sensitive ear to hear the Spirit.

We know precisely, however, that Mister Big Tom encouraged the newly bereaved father (less than a day) to take some time off from grieving. To think about God's divine Word; the Holy Bible is eternal, without beginning or end. And then, he prophesied to the clever thief; and pleasantly told him that the Holy Spirit wisely said, "You need to make up your divine peace with God this day."

This man was gifted and chosen by the dear Lord. Yet in this one instance, Mr. Big Tom ran from the Lord's divine call. He fled God's very presence, shutting off communion with the Lord.

Why??

What caused such clamant disobedience?

But Mister Big Tom's adolescent son figured out and kept to himself one staggering aspect of his dear father's emotional encounter with God (The time God spoke to him.)

Little Tom Talks:

"However, at the time I thought he might disappear," Little Tom said sympathetically.

"He also told me he continues to dwell in that dark prison cell inside the fish's belly, down into the deep blue sea; with seaweed wrapped around his head, and he is temporarily on replacement (and that is why he has disappeared from the family for a little while)."

"Then," he said, "Come on now, son, don't cry for me. I'm okay. But at least now I know."

"Although it's a dark, scary looking place with lots of loud noises. And every time it opens the mouth of hell, you hear that roaring noise. The dear souls were instantly trying to get out but could not, for they stayed embedded in the devil's belly and hell's mighty jaws."

Suddenly, an impressive silence filled the room.

Dad said, "I love you, my son, and what happened to me was nobody's fault."

"And then he vanished into the fog as I walked up toward the mirror," Little Tom said, looking at his red eyes. "

"Then, all at once, I felt very lost. I cannot say how I knew, but I knew with all my heart that daddy was gone. I felt very sad. I turned to where he had been. Sure enough, there was no dad!"

Oh, no! I cried, "Not again! O daddy, daddy, where are you?" And the darkness came and filled every corner of the room. But daddy was nowhere to be found."

TOMMY R. BANKS, SR.

Things Fall Apart:

Narrator Talks:

But as a terrible replacement, Thomas Blueberry is precisely a lonely, pawnshop salesman. He is undoubtedly having a real hard time dealing harshly with his alternative life (Instantly lost in a dark and deep sea of untold miseries that made him feel like he might drown in despair.) Therefore, it is difficult and unpleasant for him to deal in his past experience at the New Castle Town. And with all of whom Mister Big Tom was personally well acquainted to.

Ten Years Earlier:

Now, ten years before, Mister Big Tom naturally suffers an incredible lack of emotional empathy but is hit by his active imagination. He is twenty-seven years old. He struggles hard to fit into the leading role of a faithful, unmarried, reasonable man. He is mindless, cares little about anyone except himself (himself and attractive women that's all he ever cared about). He's making bad many serious goofs like flirting with lots of party girls; going out with friends and dear co-workers, day by day and night by night; hitting the bars and restaurants, night and day, no time for work, no time to pray.

More and more, Mister Big Tom and Johnny Nobody, they both drank like fish (Because of which they stumbled awkwardly in place, hollering catchwords which only they instantly understood; laughing uproariously) almost of their own accord. They smoked like chimneys, and they danced like sparkling stars (Everybody's dancing in a joyous ring around the radiant sun. 'So hey Mr. Deejay let the music play.) We're gonna cheerfully dance, boogie, till the morning light.

"And we're gonna party like its nineteen ninety-nine, but only it's not," cried Mister Big Tom joyously. So, we're going to merrily dance, dance, and dance this life away!"

Mister Big Tom's Friends and Chicks:

Mister Big Tom Talks:

"Uh, I joyfully celebrate in the most fearful time of my glorious years."

"It was a dark and gloomy day. It filled the shadowy sky with black and billowing dust. And straight through my drunken heart (at which point I garbled out loud, spitting tequila froth; for example, my mouth full of slimy saliva like a warm foamy shave) jumped out of my mouth, and I've been waiting for this moment."

"There's nothing more I can do, I think it is over," Mister Big Tom said in a slurring voice. Suddenly, I just broke up with my girlfriend, "who was known for her charming with disingenuous flattery."

She (is a vivacious redbone with a cynical sense of humor) argues that we are happy where we are and that we should be grateful for the time we have together.

"You're the only man I've ever loved!" she said, after drawing on her drink.

"I told you it's over!"

She gets increasingly drunk and maudlin, as it is revealed that both of us have suffered in a similar way.

Narrator Talks:

After they have been broken up for several days, the ex-girlfriend (Sarah the redbone) leaves town.

"I don't ever want to see him again," she said vehemently.

Lady Fair:

Mister Big Tom Talks:

And then I instantly met a career-driven girl name, Mattie. Mattie had just graduated and moves hither to New Castle Town, to work after completing college with one of my longtime friends in New York. Mattie was small but very well-built and extremely good-looking.

Joyful, Confident, and Friendly:

I moved in on her right away. Then suddenly, I was paying her a great deal of devoted attention. We were holding hands and walking together down a long hallway. And I was telling her about my big party in June while we were on lunch break. "I was wearing a gold (hip-hop) diamond cross around my shapely neck. Meantime, I put on a charming smile and gave Mattie the gold diamond cross that hung on a large chain around my well-rounded neck." My passionate performance utterly charmed her, and we enjoyed ourselves greatly. We had so much fun that day. We ended up hanging out after work and going for an early dinner.

Mattie Talks:

After hooking-up, for several precious times, I later discover that Mister Big Tom was seeing other women. One terrible night at a private party he got extremely drunk. He flirted outrageously a lot with other people dates.

A Nice Big Dance Space:

("About Thirty by Twenty")

We were sitting around a nightclub table listening to hip-hop music with a soft candle's flickering off and on. When I see Mister Big Tom talking with three women flirting while I sit along beside him, and there were people all around.

"So, now that you all are single girls," said Mister Big Tom, "how about we hit another party tonight?"

Without looking up from their tablecloths, the girls said, "We can't tonight. We got a morning service and then rehearsal. Besides, we're not a party type of people."

Mattie and Mister Big Tom Talks:

I was so upset, but his dear friends reassured me, "Don't worry about it. He really likes you."

ALIVE, I CRIED FIERCELY

Hmm, I knew in my mind something was not right. As the evening waned down, he turned to me in a social group and drunkenly slurred.

"Mattie, let's get outta here."

"I wanna take you home with me."

"Com'on home with me." Mister Big Tom asks in a slurring voice.

"Ha, yeah, doubt it." Mattie answers soberly.

"Pleassseee!"

"You're full of it."

"But I wanna be with you! I want you to come, and be with me, and stay with me. Don't come for just one night. Stay!"

"No," she repeated thoughtfully, more firmly, though in a soft voice; "I'm sorry, but I can't."

"Why not??" Mister Big Tom asked.

"Because you're wild, crazy, like some animal peering out of a burning forest on a raging fire," Mattie responded positively.

Mister Big, Big Tom Gets Mad:

He merely recites by outraged heart the classic song that Ernest T. Bass performed on the fabulous Andy Griffith show. Bass was in the woods banging on a cracked pot when he was singing in a very loud, high-pitched voice:

"Old Aunt Maria,
Jump in the fire,
Fire too hot,
Jump in the pot,
Pot too black,
Jump in the crack,
Crack too high,
Jump in the sky,
Sky too blue,
Jump in canoe,
Canoe too shallow,
Jump in the tallow,
Tallow too soft,

TOMMY R. BANKS, SR.

Jump in the loft,
Loft too rotten,
Jump in the cotton,
Cotton so white,

She stayed there all night!" (End of quote from Ernest T. Bass)
"So, you say I'm wild and crazy—huh?"
Oh! I'm drunk, am I—crazy drunk? "You, ugly face!" "Snot nose!" "Chicken butt!" and more he yelled at her. Give me my gold diamonds cross chain, and he shook uncontrollably his pudgy fist under the lovely nose of Mattie.

The Devil's Necklace:

"Gold Diamonds Cross Chain!" she screamed hysterically at him."

"Oh, stop its fine." She gently lowers her lovely head for him to take.

"Look, you can get your ugly fat gold chain. I never wanted that," cried Mattie, "howling, roaring and shrieking, as she made a rush toward the bathroom."

"OK, we're outta here! He drunkenly slurred, see you at the after- party??" yelled Mister Big Tom. Then he put the fat gold (hip-hop) chain with diamonds cross into his pocket and walks toward his friend (Johnny), slowly, knowing that he's a drunken man walking."

They head towards the bar. Johnny advises Mister Big Tom to get mad drunk and sleep it off.

"Good-bye!!!" she murmurs to herself and when she reaches the hallway she begins to run.

Mattie and Her Friend Talks:

Her girlfriend rushes to the bathroom where Mattie is crying at the sink, sobbing that he's a crazy drunk. He needs to go home and soak his stupid head."

I laughed and wrapped my arms around Mattie's neck trying to calm her down, who was crying hysterically; her makeup smeared and running all over her face.

"Oh my God, can you believe the nerve of him? Can you believe he wanted his gold cross back? I'm going to crack him in the nose!" the girlfriend whispered.

"How do I look?"

"You look great!" her girlfriend said, and then shouted, "That's it right there!" Hearing the music beat from the dance room down the hall; she headed for the door, reaching for Mattie's hand.

Mattie grabbed my hand, and without saying a word, we stepped out of the ladies' room, dancing and bobbing our heads (back and forth, while snapping our fingers) to the music.

Mister Big Tom and His Friend Talks:

Mister Big Tom's friend is Johnny Nobody, a Baptist, who was supposedly sweet and kind but was very much a hypocrite. Johnny drank, smoked, swore and many girlfriends.

My Little Chickadees:

A beautiful woman, who used to be in a romantic relationship with Mister Big Tom, left New Castle Town ten years ago and since then she hasn't looked back.

"I do wonder if she will ever speak to me again," Mister Big Tom said, thoughtfully.

"But, however, I'm still fretting over Sarah, I sent her several letters recently and I haven't heard a peep from her."

"She ignores my letters, too, the chicken head," Mister Big Tom's friend (Johnny) said with a frown.

"Hey! Why don't we call her right now? Can I use your cell phone? I have her number."

"Yes," Mister Big Tom said.

It started to ring. "Come on pick up your phone Sarah," I say. Ring, ring, ring!

"I've tried, but no one ever answers."

OK, moving right along, footloose and fancy-free!

Mister Big Tom marveled: "Oh, well now, I have seen me some sunrises; I've seen me some sunsets, but I ant never seen it put together like that."

TOMMY R. BANKS, SR.

Hey Mattie:

Mister Big Tom Talks:

"Oh, oh, I just can't think of what to say, should I go, should I stay? Just can't let her slip away."
"Hey! Mattie!!" I said curtly. She tried to ignore me but I wouldn't leave her alone.
"I wanna get to know you, baby," Mister Big Tom drunkenly slurred.
"Let's go pull up at my after party. I think we'll make a perfect couple. But you think I'm trouble. Maybe that's the reason you gave me the cold shoulder. You got me feeling like "maybe you the wrong girl." You think I'm going to be chasing a chicken butt. You don't own anything. Your toes painted, hair fixed all the time, and your Gucci boots the same color as mine. If you read between the lines you can see that I want you (holla at your boy).

Narrator Talks:

Mattie must leave the party immediately with her girlfriend, for she is too overcome by grief to do anything but climb into bed.

The After-Party:

Mister Big Tom Talks:

It was one wild evening in my small and muddy-looking shotgun house. I was in a relationship marked by my vicious behavior and recklessness (thinking about the terrible life, in which I do not want to live in isolation,) and so I decided to throw a party to end all parties. As my personal guests arrive, I meet a variety of people living on the verge of dishonesty.
A friend was drinking shots of tequila all night (he was drunker than a catfish in a whiskey steel), he passed out on my couch pretty early, amazed; he first danced around like he had scored the winning touchdown.

"Besides, several people were up and dancing around; as the music is playing, I made one more step towards the dance floor."

"Ugh," someone scoffed, interrupting my moment of innocent fun. And then I typically began to g-gg-get down on it and somebody said gleefully, "Oh look at the preacher man; you know you don't dance like that??" said one of the girls.

"He's just another Bible-thumping glory seller, aren't you?" said another.

"Hallelujah preacher!" said a third.

I smilingly shook my head, "Surprisingly, I was merely stunned, but don't really understand the logic here. It's a party! Music is playing," I responded aggressively.

"Just kidding Mister Big Tom," somebody said sympathetically.

Go Off The Deep End:

Later that evening, I was completely shocked by an unpleasant surprise. My fabulous clothes were soiled with alcohol and food waste. "I simultaneously wanted to vomit, cry and allegedly punch someone!"

After a lone night of foolishness, my friends explode and it comes to an insensate end; as a result of an episode of drunkenness. Unfortunately, I am worse than them the 'angry' drunk. I am the one who wants to discuss my 'rebelliousness' while drunk, and will not stop talking. I just want to discuss—"me rejecting God's calling on my life."

"Get me a beer! Oops! I didn't mean to do that!"

Portraying the sound of a bye gone era with a nod to the present one, he makes them realize the lesson of disloyalty is not only limited to our past.

"It is always good to fondly remember—the company we keep can typically make us or intentionally break us." Mister Big Tom said wistfully.

So—so what?? Someone answers jokingly.

"Oops! That sounds a bit difficult," someone else said shrilly.

"Huh! Don't worry your shapely head about it," it's all right?

The next morning everybody had gone home, and I have a huge mess to clean up. I check my phone and it is full of text messages from my friend's girlfriend, asking— "if he was still at my place because he never came home."

I call everyone, and no one has seen him. I decided to go to look for him along the street toward his apartment building. But headed back first to make sure I pick up all my dirty clothes, to throw in the laundry room. And there he lay peacefully, on top of the washer and dryer, fast asleep. And there was no waking him.

Then I instantly close my soulful eyes, my imaginative mind floated back to an important epoch in the apparent lack of uncompromising honesty. And there was no turning back the clock. So the key question in my conscious mind naturally becomes:

"What am I going to do while I'm here??" I whispered and continued my conversation with thinking about life journey ten years before.

And then I gratefully remembered I had previously begun succeeding wonderfully in my modern life; bonding with my nine-year-old son, instantly falling in love with my graceful and tidy wife, and working faithfully at my current job.

No Way Out:

But, as a direct consequence of my running away from God, I suddenly find myself being tormented by real life. I'm typically lost, instantly abandoned in the deep blue bobbing sea of my dear soul: "I cannot escape it; therefore, traumatized inside the black belly of a gigantic beast with nowhere to get away."

Yelling in a rage and dwelling there with an evil of every kind. Finally one of my old girlfriends (a vivacious redbone with a cynical sense of humor) argues that we are happy where we are and that we should be grateful for the time we have together.

While I am shocked by the trials, along with hardships and other complimentary extreme worries, I am finally realizing the true value of my new life. I see the gunman (Tuff) for a third time (who is now a good friend and a true follower of the Lord with an inspiring testimony to God's faithfulness!) and demands him to help me go back to my past life (as a result of which my new life is based on a misinterpretation). But while being sorrowful about my situation, "Tuff informs me that there is nothing he can do."

So, my epiphany jolts me back to my former life; on one (surprisingly) hot summer day in late June. To my loving family; to my jolly living in that notable town in New Castle, with my devoted wife and brilliant son; yet as I now realize, lonely and unfulfilled new life, on a gloomy and unpleasant summer day.

In desperation, here is an example of what I mean: Consider a chainsaw. A tool used for cutting down trees, with a blade consisting of a set of connected metal points that are driven around very fast by a motor.

Therefore cutting down trees is what it was created to do. Now imagine that the chainsaw never gets used. It just sits in the box. The chainsaw does not care.

But now imagine that same chainsaw with a soul (self-consciousness). Days and days go by with the chainsaw remaining in the box. It feels funny inside, but it's not sure exactly why. Something is missing, but the chainsaw does not know what it is.

Then one day someone pulls the chainsaw out of the box and uses it to chop up firewood, diminish old furniture, cut down some rafts. The chainsaw is excited! Being held, being used to cut down things, the chainsaw loves it. At the end of the day, though, it's still unfulfilled or disappointed. Cutting the different things was fun, but it wasn't enough. Something is still missing.

In the days that follow, it's used often. It tears through small branches, cut down big thickets. Still, it's left unfulfilled. So it longs for more action. It wants to be used as much as possible to cut down more things. It figures that it just has not had enough of these events to satisfy itself. More of the same it believes is the solution to its lack of fulfillment.

Then one day someone uses it on a tree. Suddenly the lights come on with its chainsaw soul. The chainsaw now understands what it was truly designed for. It was meant to cut down trees. All the other things it cut inadequate in comparison. Now it knows what its chainsaw soul was searching for all along.

Overwhelmingly, I realize I was created in God's image for God's praise and for God's glory. Serving God is the only thing that will finally satisfy my souls. Until I come to know God through His Son, I have many experiences, but I have not cut down a tree. I have been used for some more purposes, but not the one I am ultimately designed for, at least not the one through which I will find the most fulfillment.

Therefore, the fundamental question in my conscious mind naturally becomes:

"Why does God still want me after my destructive path of sin and wickedness?"

"But, as I said this to myself, God whispered to me: Mister Big Tom, you must go spread the good news of the gospel to all the precious people of New Castle Town.

"Go... spread."

"Spread what? Or who?"

"Spread the good news about the Kingdom of Heaven," the dear Lord said.

"So why... why do you, Lord still lack me after my destructive path?" I naturally thought and undoubtedly continued my emotional conversation with thinking about preaching genuinely scare me. Maybe I'm not good enough.

In fact, the Holy Bible tells us that even the Son of God acquire obedience through what He suffered—

"Though he were a Son, yet learned he obedience by the things which he suffered — Hebrews 5:8; (KJV)."

Mister Big Tom needs to learn that to obey is better than sacrifice (This doesn't mean Jesus had to learn to obey, for that would mean He had sinned; it means Jesus actively took the path of obedience, and then unfailingly walked in it.)

Because Mister Big Tom have rejected the call of the Lord, God has rejected him by sending an enormous beast to swallow up him who chose a selfish path.

CHAPTER 3

THE GREAT STORM

NEW CASTLE TOWN SHAKEN BY THREAT OF TERROR:

The City Of Fear

(Stop Running Away From God and Go to Work;
Seek Peace and Pursue It)

It is sultry summer, a traumatic restless nightmare in the unfortunate and gloomy city. Where you can hear the dew falling rhythmically, and the hushed town breathing without a soulful sound? It was only a matter of time before Mister Big Tom's nonviolent disobedience unwittingly brought divine punishment upon himself and others around him.

TOMMY R. BANKS, SR.

Mister Big Tom Struggles To Stay Alive:

Mister Big Tom Talks:

While I stood there on the dark and damp-looking sand in shock waves, looking out over the deep blue sea; heartily admiring the beautiful view of the shoreline; where eagles fly below the lifting surface of the flowing water; when all of a sudden the raging wind started blustering. And a massive wave seems to cover me and suddenly I was mysteriously abducted by a mighty, sightless beast. Like bustled lightning, I felt everything become dark. I found myself trolling through a state of confinement, moving around and about as death came over me.

"I was in total shock (You can tell precisely from the comprehensive look on my face that this was no joke!)"

I mean, "No joke!"

Exasperatingly, I cried out into the deepening darkness, "Let go of me; you vicious brute!"

I said fiercely, in a blubbering tone. The abundant water was all around me. At that fearful time, I instantly thought offensively, 'Now I must go where the Lord cannot see me.' But I steadfastly continued looking eagerly to him for needed help.

Begging God for mercy!!

I shouted, "Lord, dear Lord! Remember me! Have mercy on me!" I said vehemently.

Complete terror was gripping my poor brown soul, and my whole life was passing before my dear eyes.

I shouted again!

"Have mercy on me, my dear Lord! Have mercy on me!"

"I beg you to help me!!

Pleassseee, help me, O Lord of Mercy!" Mr. Big Tom screamed repeatedly.

Unexpectedly, there was a silence as I stood in the entering in of the dark prison cell inside the fish prominent belly. And behold there came a still small voice, and gently said:

"And why call you me, Lord, Lord, and do not the things which I say— Luke 6:46: (KJV)?"

> *"And therefore, do not waste any more time! And do not be a Christian that winds up in the abdomen of hell," the voice whispered.*

This might sound crazy to you, but many so-called Christians (false followers of Christ) wind up in the portal to a burning hell because of lying and doing other evil things. But we must remember that a simple lie is what caused God to kill Ananias and Saphira while in church.

No wonder great fear comes upon the dear people of this notorious town. Such order certainly has its consequence.

The hasty punishment of Mister Big Tom shows the people recognize that God's judgment has fallen on one, who by his rebelliousness had disobeyed God.

The Lord brought a furious storm on the infamous town of New Castle, located in New Castle County. Noted for its Dutch homes, commercial buildings, and gardens allow us glimpses of the rich historical history of our city. The remarkable town center with its cobblestone streets is as common as a highway, freeway, or main road. This is what makes us a unique southern community.

The notorious author, Wendell Berry (best known for "The Unsettling of America," a book-length polemic, from 1977), once said about his beloved hometown,

> *"Our history makes us what we are today, and our future depends on our past — (quote from Wendell Berry)."*

The Great Storm:

There, too, after a bit of naughtiness, there was a very loud, long rumble and impressive thunder, truly shocking impressive!

The storm itself began and for a moment it was as if everything went silent, then the shadowy skies were filled with dark and billowing dust. The wind made the sea very rough, plus the brawny storm was very strong, and our city was ready to break apart.

From the gloomy street, you could see what looked like dark strong winds coming and all this stuff started flying in the air. People on the street started screaming, and crying: babies, farmers, fishers, tradesmen and pensioners, schoolteachers, postmen, undertakers, and fancy women, drunkards, dressmakers, preachers, the neat and tidy wives, firemen, and policemen, all pointing, and yelling, "Lord, Lord, Lord, Lord, Lord, Lord."

It was terrifying. Unspeakable! Like a nightmare. Many could not control their own movements, the wind speed was unbearable. They were forced to run, to get out of the raging storm any way they could. They fell to their knees, calling on their gods, they wanted to stop the storm from destroying their city, so they began to pray and repent. They were very afraid; each one of them praying to their god, weeping and gnashing of teeth.

It Was Them Or Me:

The People with Mister Big Tom Talks:

To each other the people said. "We should find out why this is happening to us," (even though Mr. Big Tom knew it was precisely his fault).

Later, they undoubtedly discovered that the troubles came to them because of my disobedience to a commandment of God and me.

Being Picked Out To Be Picked On:

"Mister Big Tom!" the people said surprisingly.
"It's your fault that this terrible thing is happening to us!"
"Tell us, what have you done?"
Mister Big Tom told the neighboring people he was running away from the Lord. The local people became very afraid when they learned this. They asked Mister Big Tom, "What terrible thing did you do against your God?"

In response, I again use the penetrating "why" question.

Nevertheless, as a result of emphasizes my disobedience by phrasing it:

"How can God still want me?" After the mess, I have made.

Encounter with Danger:

The wind and the waves of the sea were becoming stronger and stronger. So the local people said to Mister Big Tom, "What should we do to save ourselves? Or, what should we do to you—to make the storm calm?"

Therefore the neighboring people cried to the Lord, "Lord, please don't make us die for killing him. We know you are the Lord (Father God), and you will do whatever you want." So the local people were afraid. And all of a sudden, Mr. Big Tom was taken into the overflowing water by the mighty, sightless beast. After that, the fierce storm broke and everything was calm.

"Yet, I have hope for divine forgiveness, and the opportunities to move forward without unspeakable shame and to grow more like Christ," Mister Big Tom said thoughtfully, wishing for the best; wish it for my own sake.

"Its funny how nobody wants to pray until something like this happens."

The Good Wife:

Mister Big Tom's Wife (Mrs. Liaduia) **Talks:**

"Till death do we part?" I realized this on that day when an extremely large beast not only swallowed my beloved husband, but also our joy and hope, and my good mood?"

To Be Honest I Am Not The Best Wife:

I have shouted fiercely at my husband on several occasions— when he is experiencing repercussions on behalf of running away from God, for not letting me sleep. And I have burst into tears because I have to do everything while he just lies in meditation and prayer, and agonizing over his disobedience to God.

Immediately, afterward, I feel bad and realize how silly I am. And on each one of these occasions my dear husband hugs me, and whispers to me, "I love you more."

He is not trying to win some instantly race in which we are competing favorably to see who can confess the most affection for the other.

He is simply saying that in spite of my bad emotions and foolish moments he dearly loves me more. He loves me more than he did five precious seconds before; more than in the memorable moments just before I lost my perfect wife status.

And more than the glorious day he said gently, "I do."

Married With Family:

Mrs. Liaduia, Mr. Big Tom, and Little Tom, Jr. Talks:

"Ooh Big Tom, I love you too!" Mrs. Liaduia said passionately.

This is so emotional. I was moved gracefully to joyful tears.

"I love you more," Mister Big Tom responded, with a big hug and kiss! "Thanks, I really appreciate the good support you guys are cheerfully giving me."

"Mom— Dad!" the lad yells out.

"Yeah son," they smilingly replied.

The young boy continued thoughtfully, "Since you're talking about love."

"Daddy???"

"Yeah son," Mister Big Tom answered promptly for the second time.

"Can we talk earnestly??" raise the issues of family relationships through his father's disobedience, hoping to comfort him through these difficult times.

Amazing Facts with Mister Big Tom's Young Son:

Mister Big Tom and His Young Son (Little Tom) **Talks:**

"Hours later, my young son politely tells me that he knows my secret," I asked him to tell me what is going to happen now that he knows what happened.

"Dad you're afraid. You undoubtedly have no righteous fear of God. Besides, your angriness and unspeakable terror of preaching is interfering constructively with your dear life and possible happiness. It's also difficult for Mom and me. You're totally out of control. I really don't think it intentionally hurts you physically, but I'm beginning to believe you're afraid of the people. God has called you to preach for the past days, and after the first precious time He called, you got worse!"

"You are right Little Tom; by the same token, the key issue is precisely my well-founded fear and stubbornness," his dear father replied.

"My reason for running is that, quite simply, I don't like the evil people. They are undoubtedly proud and ruthless folks living crooked lives," Mister Big Tom said fiercely.

Little Tom continued thoughtfully, "In a kindly way, the key to overcoming your madness and hatred is to trust God; for a prime example, sincerely trusting that God can bring good out of your circumstance. All these remarkable things I respectfully tell you as gentle warnings!"

"Pleassseee Dad!!"

"Open your heart to the Lord's calling now; so that you may be able to overcome your hates and fears."

Grave displeasure and fierce anger are falling desperately on Mister Big Tom.

"Well son," Mister Big Tom carefully explained, "I have gone through hell over the last twenty-four hours or so." Although I am vicariously experiencing something that feels painful, I'm being justly punished for willfully disobeying God.

I can remember having consecutive nights where I was unable to sleep. I became exhausted and very worried, for you, Liaduia, and all the dear people of New Castle Town. Which only made my condition worse," Mister Big Tom said.

Discovering the Light at the End of the Tunnel:

"I was merely in constant pain, unable to go out, and while staying in I could not ever be comfortable; terrible things were not getting any better."

Basically, the way that I saw it, was that my running away from God's divine calling made things worse. And there was nothing no one could do to relieve my terrible misery.

So in desperation, I started seeking out advice from Tuff (a villain, thief) who is now a humbly born-again Christian and a loving devoted friend, who puts others before himself.

And by the way, Little Tom, "If you see Tuff this weekend, will you be sure and tell him that I have to reconsider my learned divine calling," the dear father said sympathetically.

After some serious scares and loneliness, besides being in that dark prison cell inside the fish belly; brings not only shock waves, but reassurance; graciously allowing the genuine love of God to soak into my very being, and again finding my moral sense of calling, service and need to care.

Then, after days of meditating and praying, I noticed that salvation only comes from God. The first thing that grabbed me was that God was punishing me. This is the first time I have ever experienced anything like this. I cannot even begin to tell you how awful it was. Usually, I get very upset, or isolate myself, and do not speak when I am angry, but this was traumatizing.

"Uhh..."

"It was hell beyond hell," Mister Big Tom said in a quivering voice.

"This is awkward, huh, Dad?" asked Little Tom.

"Yeah, very," he said fiercely, still quivering.

3 Days Later:

"After three miserable days and three terrible nights, this could have been as short as 72 uncomfortable hours (reluctantly granting to a sacred almanac of Jewish news)."

(Note: when I say the "Hour," I do not mean 60 minutes. An hour in Bible times was 1/12 of the period of daylight: longer in the summer and shorter in the winter. The aphorisms in the nature of this occurrence relate to the prophet Jonah being in the belly of the great fish three days and three nights. And Jonah's historical episode is even more so substantiated by Christ's reference to it as a figure of His own burial and resurrection. "For as Jonah was three days and three nights in the whale's belly; so shall the Son of man be in the

heart of the earth—grave" (see precisely Matthew 12:40); this refers to at least 72 hours because it spoke of three literal days and three literal nights. After Jesus eats the Passover with his disciples, He is crucified late Wednesday afternoon, and His body is placed in a tomb at sundown. The next day, Thursday, was the Annual Sabbath (the High Sabbath of the Passover, which would commence at sundown), and so they could not prepare these things that day; they prepared the spices on Friday; and then resting again on the weekly Sabbath of Saturday ("where Christ rose sometime before sunset") as required. "They came early on Sunday morning to apply the ingredients" (see properly Luke 24:1), but would be greatly surprised at what they found; praise be to God, the Almighty—they saw that the tomb was empty!)

"After an entire 4,308 minutes, Mister Big Tom tie up a few loose ends in his burning head. And figure out inside the devil's belly and hell's jaws that no one escapes God or themselves."

"Therefore, Mister Big Tom figured prominently he should trust God and do what he said reverently."

"In economic desperation, he runs back to God and humbly begs to be allowed to live (enjoy) his former life again!"

Down In The Sea To Think And Pray:

I wailed out into the deepening darkness, "I do not belong here."

With sincere repentance; after running from God, I now run to God. Therefore I cried unto the Lord and said:

"I pray unto thee, O Lord, I pray to thee, give me the power to conquer all my daily life struggles of weakness.

"Pleassseee, Lord!! O God," I called out, "Where are you?" Don't let me stay here; for I'm in very bad trouble.

"Please help me," said Mister Big Tom, in a voice of entreaty.

Yes, I call to you Lord for help, and I ask that you—Lord will answer me.

Nevertheless, I am satisfied Lord with doing what you want me to do and being joyful about it."

I rolled about in the belly and cried all along. I lay in the jaws of hell in a little heap, like thrown—away garbage. Unbearable pain gripped my soul.

So, therefore, I kept on praying like crazy for deliverance, over and over again,

"Pleassseee, Lord!! O God, I called out, "where are you?"

Pleassseee, Lord!! O God, "Don't let me stay here; for I'm in very bad trouble.

O Lord Jesus, Son of God, have mercy on me, a sinner.

I am very much sorry I have ever upset you, and I truly repent, with sincere respect. I humbly pray to the glory of your holy name (in the name of the Father, and of the Son, and of the Holy Ghost) Amen."

Victory at Sea:

"Suddenly, after swimming very hard for three miserable days and there terrible nights, my humbly prayer is answered in the final moments:

"All of a sudden, I am no longer that defiant and uncooperative guy, my heart is changed. After all, the spirit of my soul which was passing away from under me clung to my triumph, convinced of my victory from the devil's belly and hell's jaws."

And then, immediately the mighty, massive beast came near to New Castle Town and rested peacefully on the white and glare-looking sand. It gave a little shudder as its prominent jaws were far and widely open. And I gracefully came a strolling forth out upon its mighty tongue on the grassy shore of my dazzling big brown soul.

Right away! God repeated impressively his supreme command:

"You will be my divine prophet. So go and preach the glorious Gospel to all the dear people of New Castle Town this day," the Lord said in a gentle but firm voice.

ALIVE, I CRIED FIERCELY

By the way, the command to go is sometimes harder than the command to stay. Many people do not want to pull up stakes and move on, for commitment is costly. It is easier to simply stay and hang about. There are many "lollygag" Christians.

However, thankfully, I willingly obeyed the holy call of God; and delayed no longer, from the byways of deepening darkness, bringing others to Him.

Therefore, I am tremendously excited about being safe once again on the relatively cool dry ground. Upon which I run home joyously, where my lovely wife (Mrs. Liaduia) and wonderful son (Little Tom) are waiting eagerly to receive me.

"Well, quite honestly, I think seriously that I am undoubtedly the lucky one," said thoughtfully Mister Big Tom. "That the imminent danger on the raging water is surely over and I'm home at completed last."

Narrator Talks:

Mister Big Tom said he was very excited, but he wasn't going to cry.

Mister Big Tom's Return, Unexpectedly:

"Surprise," Mister Big Tom said with a chuckle.

"Wow!" Little Tom said with a quaver in his voice.

"Dad you're home," Little Tom smiled, looked up at his dad grinning back at him.

"Come here," Mister Big Tom said with a wild grin.

His son rushed to hug him. His voice quivered and large tears swelled his eyes as he said to his son, "Thanks!"

The two embraced as Mister Big Tom shed a few tears, and Little Tom said, "Mom!!"

"It's Daddy! He's home!" he said enthusiastically.

"Oh my God, honey!" his wife said, as she ran from the kitchen. "Big Tom," you're really home? Thank you, Lord! "Oh baby, what happened?" Mrs. Liaduia asked, at the same time as she shouted emotionally with lots of tears, hugs, and kisses!

TOMMY R. BANKS, SR.

Narrator Talks Continue:

While Mister Big Tom's clothes were covered with bits of dried seaweed and his skin suffer a dazzling change. His face, neck, and hands were scarred with blistering-bleached scalps, from that dark prison cell inside the fish belly, and he took on the appearance of a Martian.

Reminiscences:

"Mister Big Tom went back in time to a sad, gloomy day; there he stood upon the dark and damp-looking sand, looking out over the ocean, admiring the beautiful views of the shoreline."

When the Lord swoop him up in the monster's belly of that huge fish; however, his shoulders hunched against the wind, which violently fluttered his clothes, and they went flying through the air when it struck the water with its tail.

"Let go of me, you brute!" Mister Big Tom cried in a blubbering tone. The water was all around him.

Memoirs, an Amazing Adventure inside That Great Fish:

Mister Big Tom Talks:

"Up and down we traveled towards the outside of the deep bobbing sea in a direction away from the source area, much like the rising and falling of waves caused by throwing a rock into the water; then suddenly, surrounded me as I slipped along a smooth passage of some sort. I then came into a large area marked by a slimy substance that naturally shrunk from my lively touch."

It was like a holy time out for some special thinking time; precious time to get away and gratefully recognize God.

"Once more, it threw me into the bobbing sea. The powerful waves splashed over me, and I went down, down into the deep dark sea. The blue water was all around me," but I continued looking to God for help.

"Then the water covered my mouth, and I could not breathe. I went down deep into the Davy dark where the seaweeds wrapped around my head. I was at the bottom of the sea, the place where the mountains begin; alone in that dark prison cell inside the fish prominent belly."

To Hell and Back:

Mister Big Tom Talks Continue:

"Next, I merely thought I was locked in that smoldering prison forever; but the Lord, my God gently took me out of my shallow grave. Sincerely thank you, Father God, you instantly gave me life again!"

"My dear soul gave up all hope, but then I suddenly remembered the Lord, and what Little Tom said about trusting God. So I humbly prayed to the dear Lord, and he commanded the savage beast, and it vomited me onto dry land," Mister Big Tom carefully explained.

"Wow! That's wonderful news—very powerful—indeed Dad!" Little Tom bellowed.

Return to Life:

Narrator Talks:

Finally, after three sultry days and three terrible nights in the gloomy belly of the gigantic monster with deepening dreadful gloom and visible smoke that crumbled over him. Little Tom helps his father return back to his precious family and former joyful life with a divine mission in hand. He willingly gives quick help; to instantly regain his dear father (who he naturally thought was a removable alien abducted).

CHAPTER 4

THE PURSUIT OF JOY

THE HOMEWARD JOURNEY TO MISTER BIG TOM'S RARE FELICITY:

His Remarkable Happiness

(If You Know God's Commands,
Happy Are You If You Do Them without Punishment)

Narrator Talks Continue:

Actually, Mister Big Tom wanted to say: "That's the most dangerous thing I have constantly encountered in my robust life," he naturally thought (or said to himself), "even as he begged silently—God was waiting too long!"

And when God sees exactly that Mister Big Tom is ready to listen earnestly; He gently frees him from that dark prison cell inside the observed whale's high-flying belly, but unlike Jonah, "he lives happily ever after."

Tuff smiles as he said thoughtfully, "Mister Big Tom undoubtedly becomes a much happier man, and he did precisely what God wanted him to do. He preached to the notable town of New Castle. He merely preached to this rebellious town that had run away from God, and to his profound shock, they actually listened."

At once, we instantly get to the core message of this remarkable story of Mister Big Tom. His direct response to God's genuine kindness is extremely happy! He's ecstatic:

On Cloud Nine:

"The gigantic fish cordially greeted him as he awakened, carefully making him gratefully recognize God's calling on that otherwise almost felt like a beautiful, clear mid-summer day."

Emotional Milestones:

Mister Big Tom politely told his friends that his experience had brought him a great happiness that he had never known before. He was all chummed up inside. Oh, he'd been joyous before, and happy and delighted and gratified and pleased; all those things. Of course, he had, and often, and now, he'd felt then—all at the same time. The difference now was that even though he felt all that; even though he was full in the happiest of moods, he was undoubtedly a more happy man.

Mister Big Tom Talks:

Humorous aside from desperately wanting to get back to my previous life with my dear wife and little son; I also have rediscovered the value of my faith and my trust in God's Word. If you live for Him, obey His Word and He will work for you. I sincerely mean, if you obey His Word, you can ask what you will according to God's Name and it shall be done (see John 14:14). God want you to have faith in His Word.

So then, a few days later; after reading my big, bulky Bible and praying that God might change me. And then, as by a dazzling flash, came back to my conscious mind the former life I used to live in New Castle Town. And suddenly I remembered the gentle voice of God calling me by name. In his divine voice, I graciously heard impressive power, command, indescribable joy and profound peace.

Of course, I willingly obeyed the divine voice of God. And furthermore, I have gratefully accepted the Lord's perfected plan, eagerly hoping to be joyfully reunited with my loving family.

TOMMY R. BANKS, SR.

Back Home Again:

Narrator Talks (Via Mr. Big Tom and Mrs. Liaduia):

"And now I'm home at last and my humble prayers are answered sympathetically," Mister Big Tom said gently, as he later walked carefully toward the gourmet kitchen. Wonderful smells instantly filled the private hallway. The familiar door of the private hallway gently led into the big kitchen. He walked inside.

Hungry, Cold and Tired:

"What's for supper?" He instantly gave Mrs. Liaduia a gentle hug.
"We're having spaghetti sausages and garlic bread," Mrs. Liaduia said sympathetically.
Mister Big Tom moaned, "That's sound yummy!" She comfortably wore a checked apron splattered with homemade sauce and a towel over her shoulder. She, in fact, had naturally become quite a cook.
"Mister Big Tom so glad you're home," she said joyfully, still stirring in the pot. The gourmet kitchen was extremely spacious.
Furthermore, Mrs. Liaduia said, 'Honey; what happened? What is the matter? Is everything okay?"
He said smilingly, "I'm ok."
She said passionately, "Oh, no. Oh dear god, no, Honey. Are you sure you're okay?"
He said gently, "Of course, I'm just a little tired," Mister Big Tom whispered softly; exhausted after having run so fast from the deep blue river through a nary cobbled alley between the west sides of Castle Bay."
Now, who would have thought a hot shower could feel so blissful after three miserable days of no minor showers?
"Nevertheless, upon my arrival home I was naturally worn to a frazzle. I hadn't seen my lovely family for several countless hours. I returned just precious minutes ago. Liaduia and I will soon be celebrating our tenth wedding anniversary."

My Family Is Everything To Me:

"I am my family's life as fully as they are mine. My dear wife and beloved son are gloomy but yet patient. So I sincerely thank God for those two, who are my pride and joy. I would willingly give anything for them."

'I mean anything,' Mr. Big Tom said sympathetically. Being away from my family has been hard.

I love them. I will give anything to make sure they have the best. I will spend some time with my family, before going into the street evangelization. He said they were going to do whatever Little Tom wants to do, which might include a day of video games and a trip to the movies.

Blueberry Family Fun Moment:

Mister Big Tom Talks Continue:

Moreover, the following morning, we were off to an amusing time. We have had plenty of fun exhausting one another all day. My son is a huge Ninjago fan. I like that it's a game I can let him play without needing to supervise the content.

One of the biggest things Liaduia and I liked about Lego Ninjago Reboots is that it was familiar as it ties into the first five (5) episodes of the new animated TV series "Lego Ninjago Rebooted," I also liked that this isn't a game that can be completed in an hour or two, instead you go on a mission to defend the new Ninjago city while battling a robotic army of Nindroids.

Each level features goals that you must complete to get gold bricks; each goal is achievable once you put your skills at hand. I like that the goals offer a bit of a challenge but are achievable so we won't get bored trying to complete the game. Also hidden in each level is a hidden mini-game that keeps the game fun and exciting.

Meanwhile, Little Tom yells, "Dad, Mom, I'm ready! What time are we leaving for the movie?" he asks.

"Ah, here's a movie that starts in the afternoon at 2:45," Mister Big Tom said.

"Okay," Little Tom replied.

"Alright, and what should we do after we see the movie?" Mister Big Tom asks.

"Go out to eat," Mrs. Liaduia and Little Tom answer.

"Well, where would you like to go out to eat? Would you like to go to Outback's or Rafferty's?"

"To Outback's," Little Tom replied.

"To Outback's, well, that sounds great. And then maybe we can play another game tonight. Does that sound okay?" Mister Big Tom asks.

"Yes!" Little Tom said.

A Father's Love and a Mother's Care:

Mister Big Tom, Mrs. Liaduia, and Little Tom Jr. Talks:

"Liaduia," Mister Big Tom said, "She makes sure her son knows that his father loves him." Wow. The word delivered immediately spoke with a father's love.

"We talk about Mister Big Tom every day," she said, holding Little Tom's hand.

"I remind him every day that Daddy loves you and will be coming home."

Little Tom says, "Through her love, my Mom taught me so much about Dad love for me. Thanks, Dad you're home again," he says with a big smile on his face.

"It's a family thing!"

"Yes, it's a family thing," Mister Big Tom repeated.

"Family is everything to me!"

Later, as he walks up to Mrs. Liaduia, his wife and grabbed Little Tom's hand as they walked towards the outside door. He's very excited but expressing it with characteristic silence.

"Moreover, he's happy, and so am I!" (Liaduia is also happy!) "Besides, I'm so glad you're home," she said, still walking out the living room door of the house.

ALIVE, I CRIED FIERCELY

Family Fun at the Movies:

Mrs. Liaduia and Mr. Big Tom Talks Continue:

"From the moment we arrived until we left two hours later, it was clean, popcorn was great, staff was friendly, and I was thrilled there were more facilities in the ladies room compared to the men's," Mrs. Liaduia said ecstatically.

"While spending the late afternoon and early evening at New Castle Plaza Cinema, features the web-slinging adventures of Peter Parker in The Amazing Spider-Man 2, it was the best show in town," Mister Big Tom said.

"After that, we went back to Little Tom's flavored restaurant."

Family Fun at Outback Steakhouse:

Mister Big Tom Talks Continue:

Upon our arrival, the waiter politely introduces himself as Ray-Ray; he was very friendly and courteous. Ray-Ray took time to carefully explain to us about the menu and what we would be getting. He then gave us plenty time to look through it and carefully choose our own meal. Ray-Ray took our order and when the food arrived, I was amazed how the waiter remembered who had ordered which dish without asking us.

The lovely dishes were well presented and tasted lip-smacking delicious. We all got our food at the same time; plus, we did not have to wait very long.

"Moreover, what a great day and lovely night I had spending time with Little Tom, doing precisely all the remarkable things he intentionally wanted to do," Mister Big Tom thoughtfully said coming out of the darkened restaurant.

Father Knows Best:

For a rare moment, Little Tom was blinded by the dazzling glare of the retractable headlights and confused by the incessant noises in the parking lot (incoherent sound of nature and siren blowing continuously). Then I carefully covered his shapely body with mine, and as I gently put my protecting arms around him and ask:

"Are you okay?"

And Little Tom said, "Yes, now I can see," gently slapping his hands over his ears, as we rushed back to the car. However, I guess we're off for another great game of Ninja; while the night is still young.

CHAPTER 5

OBEDIENCE:
"WHEN THE LORD COMMANDS, DO IT WITH IMPUNITY"

GOD CALLS, MISTER BIG TOM — FAITHFULLY OBEYS:

Accepting God's Law

(What Mister Big Tom did—
faithfully obeying or Accepting God's Law—Is Virtue)

Narrator Talks:

In his precious hometown of New Castle, Mister Big Tom is precisely a free man. He felt loose and alive. After swimming very hard for three fierce days and three awful nights his humble prayer is answered instantly in the ultimate moments:

And then, the mighty, sightless beast came near to the lovely shore and rested peacefully on the white sand; where it gave a little shudder as its mighty jaws were widely flung. And then, suddenly, Mister Big Tom came gently a strolling forth out upon its powerful tongue on the white dazzling shore.

Whereupon he obediently stood straightening his graceful legs and bowing his shapely head, at which he humbly prayed in a breathy voice,

"I'm sorry Lord."

"And next time I'll faithfully obey," he said graciously.

After that, he intentionally let out the steadying breath he hadn't realized he was holding dearly.

Mister Big Tom's Obedience

("A Man of Honor and Virtue"):

Certainly, Mister Big Tom faithfully kept his fulfilled promise. He earnestly warned the dear people of New Castle Town that the Lord was angry with their evil ways. And because they had seen him step out of the huge fanged mouth of (as a book of my innocent childhood wisely put it,) 'the whole big fish,' they sincerely believed what he said earnestly and did as the Lord commanded.

And when he saw it, the Lord was graciously pleased and would not smite them. Then Mister Big Tom rose up and said gratefully, "God is merciful unto us." He explains that mercy (i.e. compassion, love, sympathy, deep caring, forgiveness) is connected to God's faithfulness towards us and that: "When one feels the mercy of God, he feels a great shame for himself and for his sin."

However, thankfully, Mister Big Tom freely, willingly, cheerfully, and carefully obeyed the holy call of God with the same faith and confidence that guided the Prophet Jonah. Therefore, his philosophical perspective was always to carefully compare what he undoubtedly saw to what he knew before; as a chosen and jolly, long-married man on a (surprisingly) hot summer day in late June.

The Story of Mister Big Tom's Decision:

Mister Big Tom Talks:

As you see in the unfolding of this story, I finally stopped ignoring God. Then he firmly spoke a second time. And at the first sound of his authoritative voice, my hair rose on my shapely head and my dear heart's pounding, rushing up in my hardy throat. Again he said authoritatively to me in a really firm but gentle voice.

"So I earnestly want you to go and tell them to stop doing such sinful stuffs. I have heard about the many evil things the people are doing there."

ALIVE, I CRIED FIERCELY

"Now go and politely tell them to stop doing such sinful things!" the Lord said gently in a still calm, but authoritative voice.

"All at once, I faithfully obeyed the Lord and ran joyfully to the cobblestone streets with genuine fear especially toward God."

Besides, it would take days to walk across it or at least, it was a pretty big city full of strange, scary-nasty people. "Soon after arriving I went directly to the historic district in the center of town and began speaking to the local people there."

Narrator Talks:

At the same time as Mister Big Tom went carefully down the cobblestone streets. He most likely shared with his dear listeners the key highlights of his remarkable adventure and his virtual resurrection. No doubt Mister Big Tom, like the Prophet Jonah, bore scars from his dreadful ordeal. His shabby clothes may still have been covered with unusual bits of dried seaweed. His sensitive brown skin could very well been scarred with blistering-bleached scalps, from the sizzling belly of the gigantic beast.

Memories, the Adventures of Mister Big Tom:

For a prime example, Mister Big Tom carefully explains his mystical experiences in the gloomy belly of the gigantic whale. The sentiments expressed in this poem were that of the main character: In the Big—Bulky Whale I Cried.

The abiding lyrics by Author Pastor Tommy R. Banks, Sr., titled "In the Big, Bulky Whale I Cried." Within this compelling title, beautiful words from the Old Testament study relate to how God saves the lost the same way he miraculously saved Jonah, indeed:

"In The Big, Bulky Whale I Cried;

Gulp down into the deep jaws of the big, Bulky Whale,
I went down, down into the smoldering heat.
With white bones, and terrible afflictions at my blistered feet;
While gloomy darkness domed over me.
And all God's sunshine floats by."

TOMMY R. BANKS, SR.

"Then the big, bulky Whale instantly takes me,
Gulping down to death; therefore,
I cried out vehemently—
Into the deepening darkness: let go of me, you brute,
I said fiercely, in a blubbering tone."

"The abundant water and deepening gloom was all around me.
So, therefore, I instantly thought, now I must go—
Where the Lord cannot see me,
But I fiercely continued looking eagerly at Him, for needed help."

"Oh, my God, I wailed, please help me, Lord, I humbly beg!
Where are you? Oh, please, let me out!"

"Again and again, I cried fiercely, Lord, Lord! Save me!
From this dark sultry place, through continual—
Agony and profound sadness; which not a one,
But they that suffer can say.
Oh, I was sinking toward danger.
In gloom trouble, I called my Lord for needed help."

"Now unto Thee I humbly prayed, with sincere—
Repentance: "I'm sorry Lord' and next time I'll willingly obey."

"Right away Thou hearest my fierce cry; nevertheless,
Released my dear soul and no more in the big—
Bulky Whale, which abundantly proves,
Both wise and gentle, did I remain."
"Now, therefore by haste, me;
He rushes eagerly to gently free."

"In the gentle warmth, big—
Bulky Whale abides.
Dreadful, yet shiny, like lightening sea,
From the radiant face of my dear Saviour, by abiding faith,
God I instantly see; therefore,
No more in the Big, Bulky Whale, which,

> Abundantly proves, both wise
> And gentle, did I remain."

Narrator Talks (Via the Author):

Earlier in the poem, I warn as "Gloomy darkness domed over me, and all God's sunshine floats by; then the big, bulky whale takes me gulping down to death." Mister Big Tom now realizes the importance of his obedience to the Lord. He understood quite clearly that he was entirely dependent upon the Lord for his forgiveness and survival.

"My fascinating book forever shall record even to the end that awful, that joyful time; I look to God through the life of His Son, Jesus Christ my only Lord and Savior, my perfect example and model. I give all the glory to Him. May His mercy and divine power, abide with us forever."

Although Alive, I Cried Fiercely, and In the Big, Bulky Whale I Cried is a Christian fictional tale and a Christian fictional poem, both present a better understanding of God and the salvation that He willingly gives; I sincerely believe that many people will graciously receive the Lord—Jesus Christ once they truly understand their eternal need for Him.

Narrator Talks Continue:

Willingly let's face it; God had, in effect, raised Mister Big Tom from a certain death graciously according to our straightforward narrative. And today, considered almost everyone naturally has, like Mister Big Tom or Jonah, experienced some movable type of glorious resurrection or renewed life; graciously according to the King James Holy Bible, in the wonderful book of Romans (chapter 6 and verse 4), Paul wisely says:

> *"Therefore we are buried with Him by baptism into death, that just as Christ was raised up from the dead by the glory of the Father, even so, we also should walk in newness of life (KJV)."*

We are each called to go where God sends us—without consulting our fears—and to give a ringing testimony of God's mercy and warning. Some will not believe unless they see signs and wonders, healings and miracles.

The Leading Protagonist Talks (Mister Big Tom):

So again I shouted, "Come, God has great blessings for you!"
"The kingdom God promised you is now yours. It has been prepared for us since the world was made.
In the past, we were slaves to sin, and we did not even think about doing right. We did evil things, and now we are ashamed of what we did."
"Did those things help us? No, they only brought death."

Life, Above All:

Mister Big Tom Talks Continue:

"But now we are free from sin. We have become slaves of God, and the result is that we live only for God. This will bring us eternal life."
"When you sin, you earn what sin pays (death). But Adonai (the Lord God) gives us a free gift, eternal life in Jesus Christ our Lord."
Following the preaching in the center of the town plaza, I saw some old friends, and describe the friendship we had in my alternate life, in an effort to win them for the Lord God's glory; suggesting that they might have eternal life after all.
Nevertheless, after taking lunch and before going to sleep in my cozy upper-story Castle house bedroom, accessible by an old antique mushroom staircase, featured cypress-wood construction and a bluish-white moonroof (the morning sun beamed down on the colored slate tiles of the floor, making them look like rectangular gemstones), with its ivy-sand picture walls (upon which was very full), and was furnished with a brand new pale-brown Rattan sofa.
We placed it against the back wall toward the long, high window; so each morning when I sit with my head away from the

door, and looked earnestly forward. The first thing I saw was a high-riding, silver-bright light from the dazzling arched building across this narrow cobbled alley. But this morning it was raining hard, and suddenly it hits me, my wife and my son went grocery shopping. She likes to go early in the morning, while the bins are full of fresh food, and he enjoys all the stores.

Sleeeeeep:

And then shortly after that, surprisingly, my wife came back upstairs to our chic bedroom, while I was sleeping. "Hello," she shouted in a craggy voice; "Mister Big Tom wake up!! Why are you still sleeping? Your breakfast is ready!"

I answer in a muffled voice, "Okay, coming dear." Together with my head carefully tucked underneath the cover. When I finally woke up, I was like whoa, what happened? That wasn't a dream that was just like one of those like life-altering experiences. They trapped me inside a large, sightless beast, and it seemed like it was forever.

"I mean . . . I would never resist God again, after that," Mister Big Tom whispered in a terrible, silence voice. My head is pounding like a sledgehammer has been furiously beating my brain.

This Is Your Day:

"Good morning Dad?" Little Tom yells out, "Happy Father's Day!"

In a low tone of voice, I responded, "Thanks, Little Tom, good morning."

Jokingly, Mister Big Tom inquired, "Why does it seem like everyone is yelling?" Or, "Is it just me," he asks in a soft voice.

"Ooh, sorry Dad." Little Tom chuckled, as he sat across the oat table, waiting for his breakfast.

"Yes! Me too," Mrs. Liaduia said, "Happy Father's Day—Big Tom!" As she began to serve, she sat with her coffee cup as she watched them eat the healthy and nutritious meal she had prepared for them at the start of a new day.

"Thanks! Exhaustingly, I am weak with fatigue after consoling a father shattered by an unbelievable loss of his only son. Who was killed in a senseless shooting late Thursday night," Mister Big Tom said regretfully; as he was sitting carefully on the leading edge of his oak chair at the loaded table doing breakfast?

Thursday's Massacre:

("Murder by Mistake")

Mister Big Tom Talks Continue:

Mister Big Tom passionately continues his tragic story, drinking excessively his fourth cup of coffee. Supposedly, telling his dear wife about the horrific atrocity knowingly committed by arrested Thursday's local killer, ironically, known as Old Blue, Tuff's longtime (cellmate) friend.

"And when the astonishing news came through Friday that the local police had promptly moved in on my co-worker son's alleged murderer. It did not take anyone by joyful surprise. The mighty shock knowingly lay in the uncompromising speed at which the local police instantly moved."

By nightfall in New Castle Town's Greenway Plaza on Thursday, June 18, at 9:31 p.m., the likely death toll naturally grew another notch.

The New Castle Town has seen plenty of violence since the revolutionary cycle in 1673. What I was told about the useless Greenway bloodshed on Thursday naturally took things to a whole new level of unspeakable cruelty.

It was Saturday morning on June 20. "I am at my gentle office, busy working my butt off. I'm trying intentionally to calm a sad, broken-hearted, sincerely crying bitterly pessimistic father. Who's devastated by the senseless loss of his dear son? And why he needs salvation from the Lord Jesus Christ. "For example, however, Salvation is God's way of dealing with evil and providing a means for you to receive eternal life in fellowship with Him," I said.

"What must I do?" Mr. Jed Reston (the bewailed father) said wistfully in that weak voice.

I replied quickly in a soft, compassionate voice. "I said thoughtfully: Personal faith in Christ was the logical answer."

ALIVE, I CRIED FIERCELY

"Then finally, I willingly left after a delightful lunch, so I could get some sleep," Mister Big Tom said softly.

Home and Family:

However, after the chief consolation on yesterday, a little before apparent noon; there was precisely a huge bang in my shapely head, like a mighty hammer has been pounding furiously my conscious brain; and my whole body was tired and worn out and physically beat. "I was so exhausted I had to take the rest of the day off," he says gently.

"My frail body ached, my shapely head burned while trying mightily to comfort the grieving father over the tragic loss of his deceased son. I am washed-out by excessive toil and sweat. "And immediately upon my arrival at home; I get in bed, fall asleep, and stay asleeeeeeep." Despite having a few sounds wake me.

Narrator Talks (Via Mister Big Tom):

He said very casually, "I barely remember when my dear wife left for work last night."

However, after a long night of sleep I woke and was still just as sleeper as I was the night before. So I forgot about Mrs. Liaduia and Little Tom going grocery shopping this morning. Although I slept soundly all-night and glorious all-morning until she came in singing and shouting at the top of her lovely voice, "Mister Big Tom (Wake up!)"

Meanwhile, my naughty thoughts carefully carry me down to and through those big blue waves in the mighty ocean of my dear soul (for I was precisely three miserable days and three nights in the abundant fish's prominent belly).

Mrs. Liaduia Talks:

"Unctuously, I was so wrong to envy my husband's being able to stay home all night; because not long ago I had just finished working a second job as an overnight group counselor. And when I got home, I told Little Tom, I said, you know, it looks like we need to go grocery shopping again. After Little Tom takes his shower, he

TOMMY R. BANKS, SR.

quickly throws on some animated shorts and began carefully running joyfully down the polished stairs toward the door.

Narrator Talks:

"But it's raining! It's pouring," he said as they started out into the rain. While a cloudburst pouring its shattered pieces down on top of them.

They drove to the grocery store on the highway at the southwest side of town. There were only a few cars in the parking lot, a rainy and wet summer's morning.

They went in and Little Tom held on to the shopping cart and they moved slowly through the aisles, carefully looking, gently taking their precious time. She carefully picked up all the specific items they dearly needed, cans or cartons of organic food. And a couple of boxes of dry cereal and a quart of 2% preserved milk and some strawberry fruits; and a box of instant oatmeal with maple and brown sugar; and a box of Uncle Ben's long grain brown rice; and a box of Ramon noodle soup; and a box of spaghetti; and a box of unsalted tops crackers; and a standard bottle of dish soap, paper towels; and some canned pears, and a box of oatmeal cookies with raisins, then a loaf of delicious bread.

"Little Tom, aren't you going to get anything?" she asked, giving him a pleasant smile.

"Yes ma'am, a bag of sourer-patch candy," he said softly, grinning back at her.

"Is that everything you want?" she said quietly.

"Yes ma'am, I believe so."

At the cash register the clerk looked at the lady and said, "Did you find everything, Mrs. Liaduia? Everything you wanted today?"

"Yes, thank you, I did."

Mrs. Liaduia Talks:

"We're back from the grocery store. And now we have a church service today at 12 o'clock. Although, my husband been sleeping all night and I haven't gotten much sleep," Mrs. Liaduia whined inwardly.

ALIVE, I CRIED FIERCELY

"The church is giving us a marriage ceremony program and Mister Big Tom will be speaking," she said while they're getting dressed for service.

"Thanks, Mom," Little Tom said. "Hand me the peppermints."

Narrator Talks:

At last the rain has stopped. The sun has come up. And it's 11:23 a.m. the Blueberry family left for church (going to church was an adventure that had a much deeper meaning to them since Mister Big Tom's abduction), going to church was an adventure they now did together as a family and Mr. Big Tom promised them, that's the way it would be from then on.

Little Tom thought about his dad, their conversations, and his traumatic experience as he sat in the back seat of his Parent's Mercedes watching the deep blue sea and the dazzling white shorelines of their bewilder town pass by as if they were chapters in the life of his family.

He began daydreaming, "Things was so different now with my family. So many things have changed since dad's arrival; even the significance of his conversations has become exceptional."

"I guess I'm the luckiest kid in the whole world," Little Tom cried inwardly.

Wow, he was totally blown away by his dear father's victorious return. Meanwhile, Little Tom knew he had got too sincerely thank God for voluntarily sending his precious father back into his dear life.

Faith Alive! With Pastor Big Tom Ministry:

Narrator Talks Continue:

The noble Blueberry family walked humbly into the First United Christian Fellowship Church of Christ each with a different motivation for being there. Mister Big Tom was probably the most religious in the entire family. The only one who had officially accepted God's divine call to go out on the dirty streets of New Castle Town. And preach the good news of the Kingdom of God to the precious people of that leading city. His lovely wife knew she was there to ask forgiveness; genuine forgiveness for playing a part in her dear husband's fierce determination to run from God and her bad moods. His beloved son was there feeling a specific need to be thankful that he had never felt before in his dear life.

Concentrated most importantly, Mister Big Tom knew he was to ask forgiveness. Divine forgiveness for being such an unbridled lust filled, unfeeling, uncaring dog of a husband. He also was there to humbly ask for moral strength, splendid courage, and divine guidance for the current task he had to typically face Monday morning at his local office: "the grieving dad (a co-worker, who is so grief-stricken over the recent death of his deceased son)." And once again, it's one of those memorable moments when God says thoughtfully to you,

> "If your first concern is to look after yourself, you'll never find yourself. But if you forget about yourself and look to me, you'll find both yourself and me— Matthew 10:39;
> (The Message Bible)."

Because, God says the only way you're ever going to naturally find yourself is by forgetting yourself and properly focusing on Him. Then you'll not only figure out God; you'll also figure out you. That's precisely what it means to live peacefully like the Lord.

Pastor Big Tom's Message is a Simple One:

Mister Big Tom Talks:

Rev. Thomas Blueberry leading minister of the local church, said thoughtfully. I always begin my divine message by politely asking a hypothetical question to those in the First United Christian Fellowship Congregation of Christ; who are eagerly seeking miraculous deliverance in their dear lives?

Today was no different. I instantly begin talking about:

"Guilt- (A fundamental question for a remarkable transformation, what do you sincerely think?)" Is the unthinkable pain you have intentionally caused other dear people progressively becoming the fierce hate you genuinely feel for yourself?"

Most sensible people naturally gravitate towards one moral end of the visible spectrum of conscious guilt. On one willingly hand, some instantly see themselves as blameless and always right. Others have a tendency to beat themselves up over every little thing. If we look earnestly to God, we see that neither attitude is where he genuinely wants us to be. Instead, "God wants us to gratefully acknowledge our mortal sins and sincerely repent. He wants us to gratefully accept his divine forgiveness, turn from our meaningful ways, but then we must move forward into God's mighty will for our dear lives."

My Wife and Kid:

However, my wife, son and I have learned there are certain keys to enjoying the will (blessings) of God on a daily basis.

I sincerely thank God every glorious day that I am able to live peacefully in this notorious world. We must properly value the precious freedoms we typically have and must be accurately determined that the clever devil will never steal them from me, you and our lovely families.

There are certain Biblical keys that my wife, son and I live by so that we may enjoy God's will in our lives. I want to share with you three vital keys that will bring a greater anointing of Jesus Christ into your life.

Jesus carefully taught that the first key priority of every faithful believer was to diligently seek after the glorious kingdom of God.

"But seek ye first the kingdom of God and his righteousness, and all these things shall be added unto you
— Matthew 6:33; (KJV)."

"What is the Kingdom of God???" Mister Big Tom carefully questioned to the First United Christian Fellowship Congregation.

Nevertheless, the King James well-worn Holy Bible tells us, "It is not really the everyday things such as food, drink, and worldly possessions," Minister Big Tom said thoughtfully; as his faithful followers listened carefully to him preach the gospel.

> *"For the kingdom of God is not meat and drink; but righteousness, and peace, and joy in the Holy Ghost— Romans 14:17; (KJV)."*

So, therefore, Joy is one of the appropriate keys to successful living??" Someone from the First United Christian Fellowship Congregation respectfully asked.

"Alright!" Praise God, Mister Big Tom said heartily. And the whole church responded by saying, "Amen."

Pastor Big Tom's Message Continue:

1. JOY— is one of the unique keys to successful living:

"Don't let the enemy steal your joy. Learn how to praise God through every circumstance whether good or bad. We must learn how to be thankful, not because of what we have, but because of who Jesus is to us." Praise God!

The apostle Paul taught the early church that God's kingdom is not seen in a talk.

> *"For the kingdom of God is not in word, but in power — 1 Corinthians 4:20; (KJV)."*

2. THE POWER OF THE HOLY GHOST— is another unique key to a victorious life:

The early believers were filled and anointed with the Spirit. The Holy Ghost produced the power that released miracles in their lives. Jesus said that the precious Holy Ghost would help you in three areas of your life: "Lead, Guide, and Comfort," Pastor Mr. Big Tom said in a sermon entitled "Guilt."

And also in the Holy Bible, Jesus said:

> *"These things I have spoken unto you, that in me ye might have peace. In the world ye shall have tribulation: but be of good cheer; I have overcome the world— John 16:33; (KJV)."*

The Spirit of God is the Spirit of Truth. Earlier in this chapter— He is referred to as the Comforter. He also shows us things to come. Therefore, we are never at the mercy of the attacks of the enemy.

3. WE HAVE THE NAME OF JESUS— is precisely the final key to a successful life:

We have the authority of Jesus himself backed by all of heaven great strength. His name is our credentials of authority. The devil has to obey the Word of God. He cannot cut you off from God's love and power. That is why we need to stay filled with the Spirit of God," Mister Big Tom said, after finishing his message about 'guilt.'

Almost immediately, I saw Tuff sitting on the right side of the congregation about seven rows behind first lady Mrs. Liaduia and Little Tom. He started dancing, shouting, and praising God. I wanted to call out to him but I knew better. I got so happy that I too started dancing, and cutting a few steps all around the pulpit. I was so happy that I wasn't able to officially give an altar call.

At that moment, the saints danced and shouted even more vigorously. Overwhelmed with happy emotions, Pastor Big Tom couldn't wait to get home and call Tuff.

Narrator Talks:

Tuff hadn't felt this kind of happiness (he was extremely excited in the spirit) since the day he got saved or since the day of the robbery when he turned his life around. He couldn't wait to get home to call Pastor Big Tom. He needed to talk to him.

When they got home, Pastor Big Tom jumped out the car, ran into the house and headed upstairs to their bedroom. He was going to call Brother Tuff but the phone was already ringing.

Hello, it's me:

"Hello, Pastor Big Tom, Brother Tuff, is that you?"
"It's me, Pastor Big Tom."
"Are you okay?"
"Yes, I'm okay."

"I just want to thank you so much for that wonderful message, Pastor Big Tom," Tuff said respectfully. "It truly blessed my socks off! The tears just streamed down my face as I listened to your message. Thank you for the word, it was encouraging and powerful. It touched me so much I started shouting (weeping) and even ran up and down the aisles of the sanctuary."

Then Mister Big Tom turned and cupped his hands around his mouth and started leaping some more all around the bedroom, and shouted, "Me too, Tuff (pointing the receiver toward his wife and little son)!"

"Me too," first lady Mrs. Liaduia said (taking off her wide glossy purple hat lavishly trimmed, with her matching tailored outfit, she looked most elegant).

"Yeah, me too," said the light brown color faced nine-year-old boy (after he overheard his father's conversation with Tuff. When Mister Big Tom deliberately allowed his little son to overhear his conversation with brother Tuff, he was attempting to teach him another of his life's lessons. He knew Little Tom had a level head on his shoulders and hoped he would not be an "unreasonable person (who) goes pure raging mad when talking about the grace of God." He hoped that his son would "trust him enough" to follow the example he tried to set as a father).

Tuff Talks:

"Yes indeed, the word was definitely on point, and yes it was encouraging. I also train at a school of the Holy Spirit. Your message was definitely God ordained and truly a blessing," Brother Tuff believed.

Mister Big Tom turned again and said, "You guys are amazing in God and your love has impacted greatly in my life."

"I have been wonderfully blessed by the prayers, prophetic words, and counseling that I received from you Brother Tuff during my time of need," Pastor Mr. Big Tom said.

"I thank God for his salvation through Jesus Christ our Lord! He is the Father who is full of mercy, the God of all comfort. He

ALIVE, I CRIED FIERCELY

comforts us every time we have trouble so that when others have trouble, we can comfort them with the same comfort God gives us."

"Wow! Thank you so much!! And thanks again for your wonderful message! The word I received was amazing, rich and potent. God bless you, your wife and your son tremendously," Tuff said.

"Thanks again. Bye-bye!"

"Okay, you're welcome. Bye-bye!"

Pastor Big Tom Talks:

I hung up, and then my wife said.

First Lady Liaduia Blueberry Talks:

"Oh, God! Oh, my god!" she shouted at the celling.

"I can't tell you how many times Brother Big Tom that I have been yearning literally for a straight up message that was concrete; with no peeping around the bushes." I tell you that God spoke to you with so much remarkable clarity. Everything you said was on point. "When I heard your message, oh god, I ran around dancing, shouting (spontaneously with hand-clapping, singing), and praising the Lord."

Pastor Big Tom Talks:

For example, all that you have shared with me from God's heart confirmed many details of the visions God has given me concerning my commissioning and calling. I could go on and on. Thank you, Jesus! Thank you to first lady Mrs. Liaduia, Little Tom, and to my amazing friend Tuff!

Celebrating Our Tenth Wedding Anniversary:

Pastor Big Tom Talks Continue:

Mister Big Tom (sings), "Happy anniversary to me, happy anniversary to you, we got some miles on us—baby, but we still good as new," he said, singing out of key with a Southern accent.

"Oh, we all laughed as we continue talking about our wedding ceremony."

"That's a nice song,' said Little Tom, and Mrs. Liaduia remembered that she was hearing it for the first time."

Meanwhile, my wife and I were dreaming of a cruise for our tenth year, but the church wanted to celebrate with us and there went our plans. After an amazing, beautiful church service, we took a three-day staycation and reminisce about things that happened in our past.

A Trip Down Memory Lane:

First Lady Mrs. Liaduia Talks:

We are visiting places that were significant to us when we were dating and taking a picture of each one. We went to a movie theater we visited while dating, then hit all the fast-food joints we frequently ate at. We came home later that afternoon when my husband went into a different room; we talked on the cell phone just like the night he proposed.

We visited the church where we said "I do," and that night after an enjoyable anniversary dinner we stayed the night in the hotel where we stayed after our wedding. We watched our wedding video that night and laughed at how young we were.

Pastor Big Tom Talks:

The next day we visited beautiful unknown places in New Castle Town, and we absolutely fell in love with them. The name of our town comes from the grand arched buildings with tall solid walls and cobblestones streets (although we described New Castle Town as being filled with memories of life gone by). The chocolate gave more of a kick here, the ice cream taste sweeter here, and every time we turned a corner, Liaduia's camera would start working overtime again. It turned out to be fun, very encouraging, with lots of kind remembrances and pleasant conversations about the past.

The Ultimate Saga of Mister Big Tom:

And in my desperate journey to obeying God, experiencing Him, and finally allowing Him to take over the control of my moral life. Along with my careless submissions, my shapely head, my stubby, and somewhat ridiculous beard. They sincerely convinced me I was watching my soul float in a boundless sea of God's gracious favor undeserved love that never quits.

Temporarily, I rode inside of a whale's high-flying belly; battling fiercely every obstacle and cherishing the profound silence of every moment, before discovering the purpose of my learned divine calling.

The journey brought me through the notorious town of New Castle. And across the deep blue seas, where I discovered a wider range of real people with the same sense of purpose: "To let go (of my selfishness)—and let God (manifest His will in me)." But unlike Jonah, I lived happily ever after, more or less.

I know now why it hurried me away that terrible day without even waiting for God to answer. The gigantic fish moved quietly through the murky water, pushed by quick sweeps of its flowing tail.

Oh, it was right after that Mister Big Tom said, "Don't allow your egotism to impede you from doing the work of the Holy Spirit."

"To be thankful in everything, in all circumstances, for this is the conscious will of God in Christ Jesus for you—me," (see First Thessalonians 5:18). No matter what typically happens, or how negative things may seem to be, we are to never stop giving thanks to God.

BIOGRAPHY

Coincidentally I am a left-handed writer. As a husband, a father, a pastor, and a born-again believer of the Lord Jesus Christ with a sincere desire to carefully write about God's infallible words, the Holy Bible, and how God is working diligently with me. I mean anywhere, anyplace, or anytime; in my luxury car, during church services, typically traveling to and from fashionable hotels, or lovely cottages.

Yes, I use my philosophical writing to willingly help carefully spread the Gospel of Christ to the dear people of the World by graciously inviting them to Christ, heartily rejoicing in the sanctified word of God.

Sincerely thank you for willingly allowing me to voluntarily share my gentle words with you the dear reader. I have been made glad and blessed, so I feel sure of you that my humble joy through our Lord Jesus Christ may be the joy of you also.

JONAH: GOD'S (SELFISH) PROPHET

"Then Jonah prayed unto the Lord his God out of the fish's belly, And said, I cried by reason of mine affliction unto the Lord, and he heard me; out of the belly of hell cried I , and thou heardest my voice. For thou hadst cast me into the deep, in the midst of the seas; and the floods compassed me about: all thy billows and thy waves passed over me— Jonah 2:1, 2 and 3; (KJV)."

The lovely story of Jonah is one of the fascinating stories of the Old Testament, and it revolves around negative response. Genuine repentance is so important that God commands all dear men everywhere to sincerely repent. It is the divine gift of God.

Someone said, "I repented before I understood the meaning of the word, but since then as a Christian, I have repented many times."

This gift of genuine repentance is an inward change produced by the convicting power of the Holy Spirit as the Word of God is proclaimed. The results, repentance toward God, and faith toward our Lord Jesus Christ; faith that Christ died for our sins, and he were buried and that he rose from the dead.

Genuine repentance qualifies you for salvation, but it takes faith in Christ to acquire it. True repentance is always tied to faith. It is impossible to have saving faith and not repent.

I encourage you to read the Book of Jonah. In preparation for my request, it took me approximately five minutes to read the entire Book of Jonah. Yes, I timed myself. And by divine coincidence, I further invite you the reader to come and go with me in spirit through "Alive, I Cried Fiercely," chapters 1—5.

May Jonah be your example as you lead others to the Lord, but unlike Jonah, rejoice and be glad for the goodness God showers upon his dear people?

In his journey to obeying God, experiencing him, and finally allowing him to take over the control of his life, Jonah rode inside of a whale's belly, battling every obstacle and cherishing the profound silence of every moment, before discovering the purpose of his divine calling. The journey brought him through the bewildering city and across the deep blue seas, where he discovered a wider range of real people with the same sense of purpose: To let go— and let God.

ANNOTATIONS

As I was home sleeping in a lovely bed on Saturday, May 17, 2014, at 5:35 a.m. (CST). My dear wife gently woke me up and said thoughtfully to me.

"She had a dream that I had written an inspirational book on *"'being picked out to be picked on.'"*

Straight away, I got up, got out of bed and began carefully meditating on what to write enthusiastically. After only a few precious minutes, I naturally thought about the Book of Jonah: (eternal God's unwilling prophet) a cantankerous, defiant man, who was traumatized inside the prominent belly of a gigantic fish for three radiant days and three sultry nights.

So I wisely decided to carefully write something about *"ignoring God's holy call"* or *"steadfastly refusing the dear Lord's direct command."*

When I was seven, I became aware of the divine inspiration of God's holy call for me to preach and minister to the Lord's people. But instead, the conscious thought of actually accepting God's call scared me. So I ran, ran and ran; which means for twelve years I justly feared to do as God commanded. As a direct result, I was genuinely scared. But I finally found the courage I dearly needed to conquer my breathless anxiety. No more running. I got the well-founded fear of God!

At nineteen I willingly accepted God's holy call to preach the Gospel of Christ to the Lord's people. For me, the call came in a dream I had. I saw dear heaven open, and God seated on a very high throne, lifted up and the angels of God carefully ascending and descending upon Jesus the Son of God. I mean instantly, my dear soul was taken out of my body. I went gently with Jesus up out of my lovely bed and into the moonlit sky; it was as though I had died peacefully. And my body was left behind on the bed, while my lively spirit was going carefully with Jesus, up through to the top of the house. It seemed as though the whole roof was pulled back, and I kept going higher and higher into heaven; yet through the power of his Holy Spirit. From side to side, from end to end and from all the way through, God instantly changes me for his divine purpose; by miraculously transforming me into the express image of his—Son Jesus Christ. He genuinely wants to make me into a better and more faithful person, both on the inside and the outside.

While I carefully manage to write two small spiritual teaching books, I genuinely wanted to see if and how I could tell a story in a more far-reaching and inclusive way. I wanted to write what was in my heart—by throwing myself into a character's den. And if I have learned anything, it is to write what is in your spirit; what you naturally feel in your heart, not what you or someone thinks you should. So, therefore, thank you, wife, for naturally inspiring me.

AUTHOR'S PRAYER

From My Heart Dedicated To Yours, In Jesus' Name

"My FATHER for this cause I bow respectfully my knees unto THEE, the FATHER of my LORD and SAVIOR JESUS CHRIST. I humbly ask YOU, my HEAVENLY FATHER, to willingly give me (us) the mind, the words, and the thoughts of YOU; moreover, help me (us) to honor YOUR name by embracing YOUR' HOLY WORD.

Grant me (us) each day the things I (we) need to grow and go, above and beyond my (our) call of duty to set up YOUR' kingdom. Control me (us), and forgive me (us) of my (our) sins, as I (we) forgive everyone who has sinned against YOU, by doing evil to me (us).

And gracious FATHER may this book ALIVE, I CRIED FIERCELY, which is used to reflect YOUR GLORY on earth. It is precisely through YOUR divine power that dead soul is made alive and through it YOU direct every specific detail of unique history, for this, YOU are our GOD forever and ever. YOU will be our faithful guide even to the glorious end.

Therefore, may our spiritual journey typically begin with a longing desire for YOU? Wisely guide us that we may politely tell others about JESUS CHRIST our LORD and our SAVIOR; by HIS' DEATH instantly made a full atonement for our mortal sins sincerely thank YOU our HEAVENLY FATHER, we do humbly trust and pray in JESUS' NAME;

Amen.

—Notes—

(Specific emphasis added by Author: the key phrase, *"As we forgive everyone who has sinned against YOU, by doing evil to us."* Now, David said according to the King James well-worn Holy Bible, Psalm 51:4; **"Against thee, thee only, have I sinned, and done this evil in thy sight: that thou mightest be justified when thou speakest and be clear when thou judgest."** You instantly see, although David's mortal sin was against Bathsheba, her husband Uriah, and all of Israel; still the ultimate direction of sin, controlled by the devil (Satan himself), the adversary (or the potential enemy), is always against God.)

AUTHOR'S POEM

The abiding lyrics by Author Pastor Tommy R. Banks, Sr., titled "In the Big, Bulky Whale I Cried." Within this compelling title, beautiful words from the Old Testament study relate to how God saves the lost the same way he miraculously saved Jonah, indeed:

"In The Big, Bulky Whale I Cried;

Gulp down into the deep jaws of the big, Bulky Whale,
I went down, down into the smoldering heat.
With white bones, and terrible afflictions at my blistered feet;
While gloomy darkness domed over me.
And all God's sunshine floats by."

"Then the big, bulky Whale instantly takes me,
Gulping down to death; therefore,
I cried out vehemently—
Into the deepening darkness: let go of me, you brute,
I said fiercely, in a blubbering tone."

"The abundant water and deepening gloom was all around me.
So, therefore, I instantly thought, now I must go—
Where the Lord cannot see me,
But I fiercely continued looking eagerly at Him, for needed help."

"Oh, my God, I wailed, please help me, Lord, I humbly beg!
Where are you? Oh, please, let me out!"

TOMMY R. BANKS, SR.

"Again and again, I cried fiercely, Lord, Lord! Save me!
From this dark sultry place, through continual—
Agony and profound sadness; which not a one,
But they that suffer can say.
Oh, I was sinking toward danger.
In gloom trouble, I called my Lord for needed help."

"Now unto Thee I humbly prayed, with sincere—
Repentance: "I'm sorry Lord' and next time I'll willingly obey."

"Right away Thou hearest my fierce cry; nevertheless,
Released my dear soul and no more in the big—
Bulky Whale, which abundantly proves,
Both wise and gentle, did I remain."
"Now, therefore by haste, me;
He rushes eagerly to gently free.

"In the gentle warmth, big—
Bulky Whale abides.
Dreadful, yet shiny, like lightening sea,
From the radiant face of my dear Saviour, by abiding faith,
God I instantly see; therefore,
No more in the Big, Bulky Whale, which,
Abundantly proves, both wise
And gentle, did I remain."

"My book forever shall record even to the end that awful, that joyful time; I look to God through the life of His Son, Jesus Christ my Lord and Savior, my perfect example and model. I give all the glory to Him, may His mercy and power, abide with us forever."

Although In the Big, Bulky Whale I Cried is a Christian fictional poem, it presents a better understanding of God and the Salvation that He willingly gives; I sincerely believe that many people will graciously receive the Lord—Jesus Christ once they truly understand their eternal need for Him.

SELF-LOVE AND PRACTICAL SELF-RESPONSIBILITY

The self-love and practical self-responsibility both eagerly seeks to reflect a joyful, confident, and most friendly affection about yourself; for that reason,

"I Love what I'm doing And Doing What I Love;

FROM,
The rosy dawn of
Day; less than halfway,
Through the sultry morning of
Noon; until the deepening glow—
Of that midnight's gloom;
Surrounded by a thick,
And black night sky."

"If you believe in them,
The Creator,
And you enjoy,
What you are doing.
So, therefore, you're moral—
ACCOUNTABILITY,

TOMMY R. BANKS, SR.

Will make room for you;
And help you be successful!"

"Because it is what you do,
That will allow you—
To love what you are dutifully doing."

"It will naturally make a way for you,
When the precious time comes,
To talk of practical—
LOVE."

—Tommy R. Banks, Sr.

PREFACE

Straight from the pages of out of the belly of hell "Alive, I Cried Fiercely," there are five great chapters from scripture starring the Holy Bible's best-known character Jesus Christ, God's only begotten, Son. These independent studies reflect who we are in the life of Christ; and therefore, I am a debtor to all the people of the world, owing them the Gospel.

I believe I have been chosen to tell people the truth of the coming kingdom of God; I have as evidence the many patriots who have gone on before me, men of faith. In Hebrews (chapter 11) this is often called the "Hall of Faith." You need to go there often and linger long, that your faith may become strong in the Lord, for in this Scripture we get a view of the history of Israel and the church, as it is written by faith, in the blood of the saints.

They worshiped by faith as Abel. They walked by faith as Enoch. They worked by faith as Noah. They lived by faith as Abraham. They governed by faith as Moses. They followed by faith as Israel. They fought by faith as Joshua. They conquered by faith as Gideon. They subdued kingdom by faith as David. They closed the mouths of lions by faith as Daniel. They walked through the fire by faith as the Three Hebrew Children. They suffered by faith as Paul. They died by faith as Stephen, the first Christian martyr (Acts 7:54-60).

By faith, they were patient in suffering, courageous in battle, made strong out of weakness, and were victorious in defeat. They were more than conquerors by faith. It is only by faith in the all-powerful Christ that you can be superior to circumstances and victorious over all the evil forces that would destroy you. "**Looking unto Jesus the author and finisher of our faith-** (Hebrews 12:2a)." The faith of the saints inspires me, but I look to Jesus as my example of faith.

So I hope this book will challenge and encourage those who profess to serve the Lord and also introduce the vitality of repentance—yes, repentance is so important that God commands all men everywhere to repent. It is the gift of God.

This gift of repentance is an inward change produced by the convicting power of the Holy Spirit as the Word of God is proclaimed. The results, repentance toward God, and faith toward our Lord Jesus Christ—faith that Christ died for our sins, and He were buried and that He rose from the dead. Hallelujah! Repent now before it is too late.

DEDICATION

To my dearly loved Mother: Sarah Lee Banks, for the dwelling inside the belly and through my stunning disquietedness passed out into a life of faith in progress, with trials and successes, times of reflection and of fun, thanks for all your affections.

To the late adored Pastors of my youth: Reverend Washington, thank you for being my first pastor; and Reverend Walter Lee Debro, Sr., thank you for preaching the Word. I believe the Word today because you and the church you led gave me that grounding.

On behalf of *"Alive, I cried fiercely,"* I would like to thank you both for all your teachings this experience has already increased my desire for a never-ending relationship with God.

A special dedication to the late Honorable Judge L.T. Simes, to my wonderful mother-in-law Dianna Layne, to my late, dearly missed father-in-law Eddie James Thomas, and to those who are displeased and disappointed may this book be an encouragement to you. To those who are busy making things happen, may this book be an encouragement to continue. And to those who are unaware of what's happening, may this book provide as a tool in the appropriate place.

ACKNOWLEDGMENTS

Thanks To

Thank you to my son, Tommy R. Banks, Jr., for the sacrifice of time you carried during this five-year process of completing this book.

I cannot adequately thank my wife, Wanda L. Banks (Lady B), for her constant love, encouragement, advice, input and editorial guidance. You carried a heavy burden during these five years of my writing. I love you.

Sincerely thank you to my parents (aka momma em) Sarah and the late JW, my likely siblings. My dearest cousin Prophetess Renda Horne has authored two published books entitled, **"Seven Years in Egypt; Seven Years in Egypt- recognizing your setbacks as set-ups for your comeback,"** my dear friends, and to all these kind people; beloved Mentors, Pastors, Predecessors, Teachers, and Parishioners.

Sincerely thank you to the former Mayor of Como, Mississippi, the Honorable Azria "Bobby" Lewers, for all your support.

Heartily thank you to the Rev. Dr. Booker T. Sears, Jr., my Pastor, and local spiritual advisor, during my college days; the legendary Pastor of the Good Will Baptist Church, Bronx, NY., a great theologian of the well-worn Bible. Sincere thanks for all your brotherly love and hearty support; willingly giving me the incredible opportunity to preach the Gospel of Jesus Christ to the local congregation and honored Tuesday's fellowship ministry.

TOMMY R. BANKS, SR.

Above all, I sincerely thank God, my Father, for my Lord, and my Savior Jesus Christ who has willingly provided the earnest desires of my dear heart in enabling me to properly complete this remarkable book.

ABOUT THE AUTHOR

Tommy R. Banks, Sr., has served as pastor of Progressive Baptist Church, Harlem, New York. He has faithfully served as a law enforcement professional; and has gratefully received official recognition and distinct honor at the local police officer's annual awards ceremony in Marshall County. He joyfully received the doctor of divinity degree (in Religious Studies) from Tennessee School of Religion Seminary. His doctoral dissertation appropriately titled "A Study of the Christian Faith of hoping from the Perspective of the hearty way an African American Person or Black Church Thinks."

ABOUT THE BOOK

There are five great chapters from Alive, I Cried Fiercely, starring the best-known character Thomas Blueberry, also known as Mister Big Tom. These independent stories relate to how God saves the lost the same way he saved Jonah.

It present a better understanding of God and the salvation that He willingly gives; I sincerely believe that many people will graciously receive the Lord—Jesus Christ once they truly understand their eternal need for Him.

So I hope this book will challenge and encourage those who profess to serve the Lord and also introduce the vitality of repentance—yes, repentance is so important that the Lord God commands all men everywhere to repent. It is the gift of God.

LOOK FOR THESE OTHER BOOKS
BY TOMMY R. BANKS, SR.

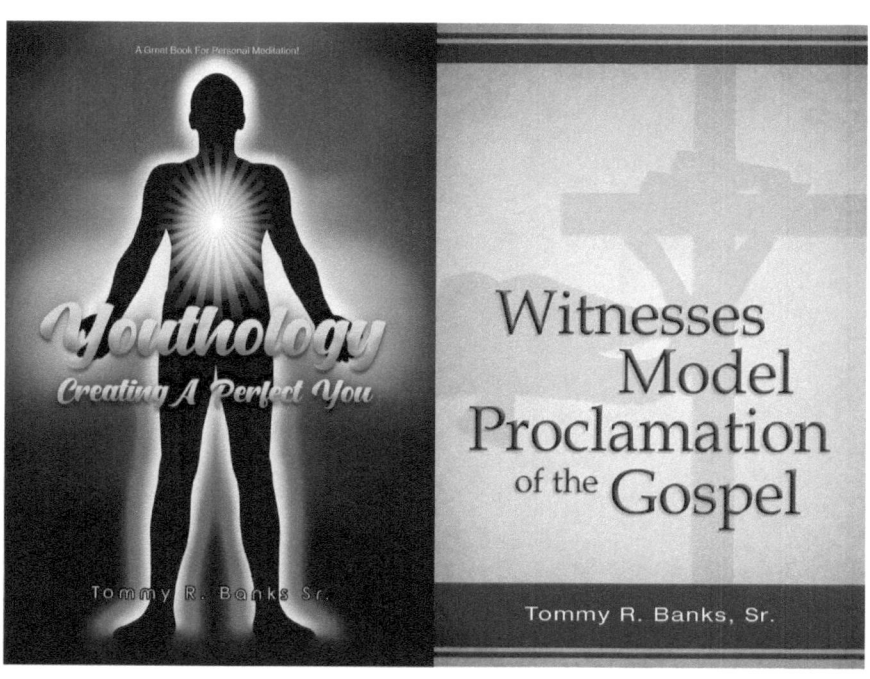

In Loving Memory of
Sarah Lee Collins-Banks
April 22, 1943 — September 29, 2019
The Lord is my shepherd....
Psalm 23:1

www.ingramcontent.com/pod-product-compliance
Lightning Source LLC
LaVergne TN
LVHW091557060526
838200LV00036B/884